The Megawind
Cancellation

The Megawind Cancellation

Bernard Boucher

Atheneum

New York

1979

Library of Congress Cataloging in Publication Data

Boucher, Bernard.
    The megawind cancellation.

    I. Title.
PZ4.B754Ml 1979 [PR6052.0795]   823'.9'14
ISBN 0-689-10947-4   78-72977

The Megawind
Cancellation

Chapter One

Now the narrow ribbon of road ahead dipped and twisted through round-topped, jungle hills.

He was fully alert, working at the wheel, easing a hundred feet of swaying, roaring road train round tight alternating bends as the solitary strip of bitumen weaved its way towards the wooded mud-flat shores of Australia's northern coast.

Maintaining momentum, that was the secret. A moment of inattention, a falter of the nerve, even a slight relaxation of his attack on the road, and speed would be sapped from his wheels as he lifted from a gully, forcing him down perhaps ten gears. Such errors cost time and fuel and sweat. Ray Mead didn't make them. He was a pro, the best. So seventy tons of towering truck blasted open the bends at 50 m.p.h.

They had done a good job on the old military highway linking Alice Springs, deep in the red heart of Australia, with the isolated tropical seaport of Darwin. The Allies had built the road as a national defence artery during the Second World War when the Japs developed the habit of bombing the northern outpost. When the war was over, Darwin found quite suddenly that it had become part of the Australian continent, linked to the railway network in the south by a thousand miles of sealed highway.

Over thirty years the narrow strip of road had been resurfaced and improved repeatedly until today it was grand enough in sections to sport a white line down the centre, but, when it wound its way through the olive-green hills south of Darwin, it remained a single, gravel-edged track full of turns and treachery.

He was still in open range country where cattle

roamed free, hell to travel at night and little better at this time of day with the sun coming up and animals on the move. Round a bend could be a pair of wild buffalo, standing in the middle of the bitumen, staring blankly between great horns at the approaching din. Hitting one was like running into a wall. They could buckle the sturdiest kangaroo bar back into the radiator, bloodying the windscreen in a sudden moment of death.

The roadside was littered with the stinking fly-blown corpses of cattle and kangaroos, thrown aside by impact, while smaller creatures, the native cats and the lizards, were simply flattened into the tarmac. Feeding birds flew hurriedly up from the bodies as he approached. Eagles, hawks, parakeets, cockatoos. Sometimes a whole flock of parrots would scramble into the air in a colourful spray, the stragglers and the hungriest delaying too long, bouncing off the front of the truck, suddenly limp, to add fresh meat to the highway fodder.

When a small, grey wallaby skipped into the road ahead of him and froze, stretched full height to watch the approaching vehicle, Mead's foot stayed firmly pressed on the accelerator.

Maintain momentum.

The animal turned and bounded back into the undergrowth, hidden from sight by the time the truck reached the spot where it had stood.

The fast-growing tropical bush pressed hard on the highway, accepting its intrusion in a hot, moist embrace. Grazing cattle could remain hidden by the roadside vegetation until it was too late to avoid them when they strolled with nightmare slowness into the path of a speeding road train.

'Like driving through a bloody zoo,' Mead complained aloud to himself. It was a habit one developed on a lonely road.

Some of the truckies ran their business so close to the

edge of bankruptcy that a collision with anything bigger than a wildcat could be the final straw that broke them. The nearer they got to financial disaster, the harder they drove themselves until one day, dazed and wide-eyed from too many pep pills, they rounded a corner and ran slap-bang into the inevitable.

Not Ray Mead. He was no mug. He wasn't going broke, and he didn't shoot beans to stay awake. He made sure of four or five hours' sleep every night he was on the road so that now, four days out from Adelaide and nearing the end of the gruelling two-thousand-mile haul from the southern coast, he was fresh to concentrate on its most dangerous section.

A thousand miles back, in the dusty vastness of the desert track, he had been able to relax. A man can dream all day at the wheel out there with not a tree between him and the wide horizon, and the road, straight and featureless, stretching empty ahead for miles until it disappears into the distant haze of heat.

Here he had to stay sharp, tensing at every corner in readiness to meet head-on another road train heading south or one of the long, linked tankers running fuel down to Katherine and Alice Springs. He had to slow down and move half off the road for them, but there was no way in the world he was going to shift off the bitumen for an oncoming car. The locals knew it and pulled on to the dirt to let him pass, but the tourists expected him to share half the hard surface with them and kept two wheels on the road until the last second when they realised the massive truck demanded the entire width. He drove straight at them. His speed never slackened. It amused him to look down on their frightened faces as they swerved violently into the endless line of empty beer cans tossed out by thirsty travellers and slid to a halt as the rush of his trailers showered them with stones and dust.

He was making good time. Hayes Creek was round the next bend. A few months ago, arriving here this early in the morning, he would have pulled in for a sizzling breakfast of steak and eggs. It was one of the best watering-holes on the road, a solitary roadhouse sitting on top of a hill above a creek just filling with the first of the season's rain.

Old Grunter's truck was standing at the petrol pumps. The miserable bastard would be in there moaning about the potholes, feeding his fat German face and eyeing the waitress's legs. Mead wondered if the same girls were there. He had had some wild nights at Hayes Creek. He promised himself he would call in on the homeward run. Today he had to pass it by.

The blackened, twisted wreck of the burnt-out fuel tanker was still at the bottom of the hill, the almost unrecognisable remains of its prime-mover and trailers sprawled on their sides in charred scrub.

What a show that had been! Some little Italian joker, new to the road, had parked eighty thousand dollars' worth of fuel and road train outside the bar while he went inside to wash the dust down his throat. He was just sinking his first can of beer when, behind him, the whole damn load quietly started rolling off the top of the hill. It must have been doing a fair lick by the time it left the road, sailed over the cliff and exploded with an almighty bang which started a raging bushfire. The poor sod walked slowly to the door and stood staring at the flames. 'You might as well have another beer, mate,' said the barman. They say the little bloke didn't sober up for a week, and the fire was last seen three days later going over a hill ninety miles away.

Mead grinned at the thought of it. He could just imagine the look on the bloke's face when it dawned on him that all the noise might have something to do with his tanker. It was one hell of a way to quit a job! At least some of his outfit was still on the road, riding in the dabs of a dozen truckies like Mead who had listened to the barman tell the story for the hundredth time, then walked down the hill to collect a weirdly twisted fragment of gleaming metal as a souvenir.

He wound down the window to see if he could get a sniff of breakfast cooking, but all that came in was the sweet warm smell of the bush. Maybe he would have had some mushrooms too, and a few fried tomatoes spread around the plate.

No good thinking about it. There was no stopping this trip.

He closed the window before he lost all the cool of the air conditioning, and lit a cigarette, trying to forget his hunger.

Neil Diamond, that would help! He reached through the curtain across the bunk behind him for the box of cassette tapes, hooked one out and pushed it into the slot in the tape deck.

He used the stereo more than the radio on the road. Most of the way, he was out of radio range and, when he could pick something up, the atmospherics made it hardly worth hearing.

Yes, he had a smart unit all right. It was only six months old when he bought it a year ago. Thirteen forward gears, a 335 h.p. motor hauling two trailers with nine axles, and thirty-four tyres on the road.

In large yellow lettering across the front fender the words 'Road Train' issued a clear warning to other traffic. He was proud of that emblem. It gave him priority and status on the road. In a way it was like a medal. It declared him as a master of the meanest, toughest highway on the continent. Each morning on the road he would wipe the red dust from the wording on his cab doors: 'Ray Mead. Interstate Haulage'.

He was not doing badly for a guy of thirty-two with a

wife and two kids to feed. Next month he would finish the repayments and the whole set-up would be his, lock, stock and barrel.

A crude signpost on the left pointed down a wide dirt track to the Daly River Aboriginal Reserve.

Mead glanced at his offside mirror and saw a car nosing out behind him. The road was wider here but still not broad enough for them both on the bitumen. He pulled over until the nearside wheels were running on the dirt and flashed his offside indicators a couple of times to signal the car to pass. With only a few miles to go, he did not want anyone sitting behind him. He looked down on the roof of the car as it silently overtook him, the sound of its engine drowned out by the roar of the truck.

A flick of a switch on his central control panel cut in the automatic engine brake as he studied the road ahead for familiar features. That was the trouble with this damn scrub. It all looked the same. He kept an anxious eye on his mirrors, but there was no sign of other traffic.

Suddenly he realised his stomach was tense. What the hell was he nervous for? He had done this half a dozen times before.

The road dipped and swung to the left. On the right a large group of man-sized ant hills rose like a marauding gang from the white grass in a clearing. The truck slowed and Mead moved into a lower gear range.

When the track appeared ahead he took a final look at his mirrors before swinging off the highway. The surface was firm but the track was narrow as it left the bitumen at an angle of about forty-five degrees. The pallid green leaves of scrappy eucalypts brushed against the sides of the truck, springing back into place as it passed. The track curved to the left and started to climb through the trees. Mead cursed as he fumbled a gear change. He hated doing that, but it happened to the best of them. At the top of the rise the track widened and he could see parts of some old bitumen, cracked and latticed with grass but still resisting the perennial onslaught of nature.

Another half a mile, and the truck rolled out into a vast tree-lined clearing. Down the centre ran a long-abandoned airstrip more than a mile in length with taxi-ways leading off into the scrub.

Mead brought the truck to a halt with a hiss of air brakes, flung open his cab door and swung himself out on to the top foot rung. He studied the tops of the trees for a moment, then looked back down the runway. There were some cattle wandering across the far end. They were the only sign of life apart from the birds breaking from the tree-tops, circling and plunging back with harsh cries of warning.

Satisfied, he got back into the cab and drove the truck down the middle of the black bitumen airstrip towards the distant cattle. They strolled away listlessly as he approached. He wound the road train round in a loop on the apron at the runway's end and stopped close to the fringe trees where a series of rectangular concrete bases marked the sites of buildings long since removed.

He switched off the engine and lowered himself to the ground, suddenly engulfed in the clammy heat of the bush. After the coolness of the air-conditioned cab it was as though he had dropped into a warm pool. In the stillness, without the familiar roar of the motor, he listened for a while to the vibrant sounds of the jungle. The sudden ringing call of a bell-bird sounded nearby above the shrill, persistent rasp of cicadas. He felt strangely alone.

Mead glanced at his watch. It was just before ten o'clock. Time enough for him to have that breakfast he had been thinking about. He had been on the road for six hours without as much as a cup of coffee. Following a well-ingrained habit, he walked along the trailers, checking the load and bending to run his hand across the surfaces of the tyres. He had saved many a blow-out by stopping every hundred miles or so to pull out embedded nails and bits of wire before they ripped the casing to pieces. Most times a flat tyre meant a new tyre unless it was the inside one of a pair and the load distribution prevented it from being ground into the road. Wheel-changing was a daily chore. With the wheels running in groups of four, the rear pair could be impaled by even a flat, blunt piece of steel when its end was lifted from the road by the weight of the front runners. He carried eight spare wheels and, when they were all used up, he had to start repairing punctures on the roadside. Regular check stops had saved him a packet. Those tyres were worth two hundred apiece so a few flats could soon drain the profit from a run. The pill-popping idiots would go roaring on, thinking they were making good time, and the next thing they knew hot rubber was flying or the load had shifted and the whole bloody trailer turned over at the next bend.

Two of the chains holding a towering stack of concrete pipes on the rear trailer had worked a little loose. He took a length of steel tubing from one of the lockers and climbed on top of a wheel to insert it in the ratchet. He heaved on the end of the bar and the ratchet clicked twice as the chain bit deeper into the rubber cushion over the top pipes. A deep breath, and he heaved again, muscles tightening under bronze-tanned skin, the whole weight of his body hanging from the lever. He might have been short, but years of trucking had given him the strength of a weight-lifter. His light blue singlet darkened with the moisture of his sweat. Tight enough. He repeated the operation at the other end of the forty-foot pipes. No sense in strewing Darwin's new sewers all the way along the Stuart Highway. He dropped to the ground and rubbed his hands on his shorts.

At the front of the leading trailer was a large cream-coloured compartment, spattered like the pipes with the red mud of the desert. With familiar ease he lifted himself on to the trailer. Unlocking the padlock, he slid back the steel door of the compartment to be greeted by the raucous cries of the birds. He walked inside and started lifting crowded cages off the fiddled shelves, lowering them to the ground on a hooked-pole. A sulphur-crested cockatoo, white and yellow and wide-eyed, tried to take a chunk out of his finger and he dropped the cage instinctively, spilling seed and water from the troughs and piling the birds together in a squawking, frenzied heap.

He talked to them as he lifted them down, as though he could calm them with the sound of his voice. Yes, they were beautiful all right, even the tiny ones fluttering across the cages in colourful confusion.

Soon there were sixty cages sitting on the baked, brown ground. From a tank slung under the side of the leading trailer, he filled a watering can and started topping up the water in the troughs, pushing the narrow rubber filler hose on the end of the spout through the bars.

He counted forty-three dead birds. Most of the bigger ones lying at the bottom of the cages were crimson rosellas and pink Major Mitchells, birds he saw daily in great flocks along the road. But one was a large, noble-looking bird with striking golden plumage that caught the eye even though it now lay lifeless.

Mead knew little about birds. It looked like some sort of parrot, and it looked important. He could not see another like it in the other cages. Someone was not going to be happy about losing that one, he was sure.

He would have to do something about enlarging those air vents.

To hell with the birds! He'd eat first and clean up the bodies later. He had plenty of time.

He lit a small fire on one of the concrete bases, took a couple of eggs and a slice of steak from the refrigerator at the head of his bunk and dropped them into the frying-pan he had placed on a stand over the flames. He lowered the side of a trailer locker until it was held horizontal by retaining chains so that it served as a table. From the top of the locker he took a small, folded canvas seat.

The breakfast bar, he called it. He didn't quite go to the extent of having a tablecloth, but everything else was there to enable him to eat in civilised comfort. Cereal, condiments, sauce. The cutlery was sorted carefully into the appropriate sections of a divided tray, and containers of coffee, tea and sugar held in place by clips.

He liked to do things in style. Let the other mugs chew on a chunk of cheese and a loaf of bread all the way from Adelaide to Darwin if that was the way they wanted it. Most of his life was spent on the road, and he didn't intend to live like a slob. It was too easy to let yourself go, ignoring the sweat-caked dust in your hair, the grease stains on your skin and the stench of your own body in the cabin. So most mornings when the cages were not full of squawking birds he stopped at a service station or one of the watering-hole bars for a quick shower and a shave. It paid off.

Sure there were some rough tarts on the road who didn't mind rolling in a bunk with an ape, but there were some classy dolls too, English girls, and Swedes, and Yanks, doing their world trip independence thing on cheques sent out by mummy and daddy. Some guys would slip them a couple of beans to turn them on. Mead did it with style. Dinner under the desert stars, and a bottle of the best wine. Then they'd screw.

He washed up the breakfast things and turned his attention back to the cages, cautiously reaching inside to take out the dead birds. He threw the bodies on to the fire, then carefully swept the feathers and dust from the compartment floor into a dustpan and emptied it into the flames.

Occasionally he glanced at the sky, now filling with huge white columns of puffy cumulus, but there was no movement apart from the floating forms of the kite hawks hovering high on invisible currents.

He looked at his watch. It was just before midday.

From under the mattress on his cabin bunk he pulled a large square of luminous yellow plastic which he spread out on the tarmac at the end of the runway.

The plane came in low from the west. It circled the strip, passing right over the truck before making its landing approach, touched down at the far end of the strip and taxied towards him. The long-distance fuel tank on the port wing swung to within a few feet of the rear trailer as it rolled to a halt.

As the engines died, Mead was hauling a fuel line towards the aircraft. He opened the fuel port in the far wing, inserted the hose nozzle and ran back to the trailer to start hand-pumping avgas from one of the forty-four-gallon drums. The pilot was already unloading empty bird cages from the cargo door.

'Any problems?' he called without pausing in his task.

'No worries this trip, but those creeks are filling,' Mead told him. 'That road could be cut at any time, and then it's going to stuff up our time schedules.'

' You'll make it. How many you got this time?'

'Six or seven hundred, I'd say.'

'Well let's get them on board.'

The pilot started lifting the birds into the plane. By

the time Mead had filled the port tanks, he had stacked all the cages into the fuselage. While the truckie was rewinding the hose, the pilot checked the fuel, draining some from each tank into a glass jar to see if there was any water in it and throwing the sample out on to the tarmac.

He unlatched a locker behind the starboard engine and took out four new-looking grey attaché-cases, identical to four Mead had brought over from the truck.

'Just be sure you're here next time,' he told the truckie as they exchanged the cases.

He looked around anxiously.

'And clean up all signs of that fire.'

Mead was irritated by his manner. He was a cocky young bastard. He could just imagine him living it up like a lord on Bali, ordering the natives to run and fetch for him and conning their best-looking girls into bed. It was difficult to resist the temptation to smack him on the ear.

As Mead pushed the fresh consignment of attaché-cases up on to the truck passenger seat the plane's engines revved to a flying drone and it went straight into a take-off.

He glanced at his watch. The whole change-around had taken less than twenty minutes.

He stacked the empty cages into the trailer compartment, poured water on the remains of the fire and swept the concrete clean. A final check, and he climbed into the cab.

He smiled to himself as he pushed the cases into a locker above the bunk. Another five thousand dollars to put in the bank! Not bad. Not bad at all for a delivery boy.

The problem was that they had no idea what the road was like. How could he ever be sure of making a pick-up on time?

He jammed his thumb down on the starter, and that sweet motor burst back into life. The big truck turned back down the runway, its twin image merged to sharp clarity in the binoculars trained on it from the hill.

Chapter Two

Mike Lindsay took a deep breath and jumped, thrusting his feet down hard on the rail to propel himself well clear of the side of the ship.

A moment of breathless suspension, the night air flowing cool on the sweat of his face, then he pierced the flickering reflections of the wharf lights on the water in a sudden engulfing turmoil of bubbles. He kicked his way back to the surface, gasping from the force of the impact and the unexpected coldness.

It was a hell of a way to disembark.

A bullet smacked into the water close to him. He looked up and saw two shadowy figures on the wing of the bridge. One was gesticulating excitedly and shouting. The other was hunched over a rifle, waiting for Lindsay's head to bob into a patch of light. Behind the ship the great arch of the Sydney Harbour bridge curved away into the night, lit up like a Christmas cake with a red beacon cherry on top.

This was no time to admire the view. Lindsay surface-dived and swam with long, smooth strokes towards the dark length of water along the side of the ship. His sweeping hands touched the hull, and when he eased himself cautiously to the surface again he could no longer see the crewmen.

He could have sworn that thick-skulled skipper was out cold when he left him. He had hit him hard enough. But somehow the tough little bastard must have reached that intercom and raised the alarm. Thank Christ most of his crew were still ashore, no doubt perving through the peep-shows up at Kings Cross or making their own little Asian contribution to the spread of international friendship and venereal disease! If they hadn't been, he would never have made it to the side. Then there would have been hell to pay.

Lindsay swam towards the stern of the ship. Breast-stroke. Nice and easy. No ripples.

He could hear more shouting above him. They had a light that was skipping across the water in a frantic search. He was glad of that. It told him how far away from him they were looking.

He reached the stern of the freighter and paused to study the open stretch of water between it and the dark shape of another rusty old cargo ship at the next berth. The gap was too well lit to risk swimming across on the surface, and it looked too wide to cross underwater.

Two figures ran along the wharf and stopped silhouetted against the freight sheds to peer down between the ships. Behind Lindsay the probing light traced his course.

He sucked air deep into his lungs and submerged, striking out towards the other ship. The clothing didn't help. He had no hope of making it in one.

When he surfaced in the open water, the silhouettes had gone and the light was still searching the dark shadow of the Vasendra. He promised himself he'd sigh with relief when he got his breath back.

On the debit side of forty, and twenty-a-day, a man can use a bit of luck!

He reached the other ship with the next dive and worked his way along to the stern which was tucked into the corner of the quay. From there he swam across to the opposite wharf, ignoring inviting iron ladders rising from the water until he found one hidden behind a Norwegian freighter on the far side.

There was no one around when he poked his head over the top. He sat on a bollard to pour the water from his shoes and peel off his socks, watching the open end of the quay for any movement.

The car was parked well out of sight of the Vasendra. He walked to it barefoot, shoes in hand. A quarter of an hour later he was driving through the busy late-night traffic of Sydney.

Crowds were still thronging the footpaths of the Cross, filtering through the sex shops, bantering with the touts soliciting customers for the adult movies and strip shows. Hamburgers and hot dogs, neon lights and whores.

Lindsay sat in a two-way traffic-jam watching the midnight sightseers weaving through the cars and wondering what perversity compelled him to live in a Kings Cross terrace instead of a leisurely beach suburb or on the banks of one of those exclusive, wooded coves in the back reaches of the harbour.

He could not even find a parking place outside his own front door.

One of the girls was leaning against the railings as he walked down the street. She studied him curiously as he approached, rattling the keys in her hand instinctively.

'You been swimming, Mike?'

'No, darling, I just sweat a lot,' he grinned.

She ran a hand over his shirt.

'My, my! You are wet. You'd better get those things off before you catch your death of cold.'

That was one of the reasons he lived here, he remembered. He had such friendly neighbours.

An envelope fell at his feet when he opened the flyscreen door to put his key in the latch. He switched on the lounge light, glanced at his name on the envelope and ripped it open. It contained a ticket for the 8.30 a.m. flight to Canberra and a typically uninformative message from Alan Coates.

'See you in my office 11 a.m. Bring toothbrush. Coates.'

Lindsay took a closer look at the ticket. Coates had

23

booked him first class. At least he would get some breakfast on the plane.

Lindsay paid off the cab outside the Woolshed.

No one knew who had first given it that title, but it was appropriate enough.

In the architectural elegance of Canberra, amongst lofty new government offices surrounded by green tailored lawns and banks of floodlights, the Woolshed hid itself well away from the road behind ragged, peeling gum trees. There was nothing to distinguish it at a distance from the other drab, two-storey fibro huts lined in rows across brown, dusty grass with all the aesthetic appeal of a hurriedly-built army camp.

He felt an old affection for the place as he walked towards it. The same public service cream paint was flaking from the walls in the hot summer sun, and the grey-pebble garden, a post-war apology for the absence of landscaping, looked even scruffier than the last time he had seen it. It was still growing filter tips he noticed.

At least the signboard outside the door remained readable—'Department of Customs and Excise. Unit 3'.

He smiled to himself. It was about as communicative as the men who worked there.

Lindsay went up the stairs two at a time and turned down a dark, echoing corridor, passing through a door marked FEDERAL NARCOTICS BUREAU. The corridor continued beyond the door, with anonymous offices strung along both sides. From one he heard the chatter of a telex machine as he passed. He pushed open the next door on the right and went inside.

A new girl was at the typewriter. She seemed to resent the intrusion. Lindsay was tall, dark but not exactly handsome.

'The director's busy at the moment,' she told him.

24

'Please take a seat, and I'll let him know you are here.'

He sank into a comfortable armchair and started flicking lethargically through an old magazine.

He did not have to wait for long. The inner door opened and Alan Coates walked across to him with hand out-stretched.

'Mike Lindsay! Good to see you. Come on in.'

The receptionist looked surprised, for the first time showing a mild interest in the visitor.

A lean-faced man in a fawn-coloured safari uniform rose from his chair as they entered the office. Lindsay took a quick look at his circular shoulder-flash, but it didn't mean anything to him.

'Mike, this is Senior Inspector Jamieson of the National Fauna Squad,' Coates told him.

Jamieson shook hands with Lindsay as Coates completed the introduction. The bureau chief lowered himself into a black leather swivel chair behind his desk, indicating Lindsay to sit opposite him.

'I'm sorry about the short notice. I tried to contact you earlier yesterday but nobody seemed to know where you were.'

'I went for a swim.'

Coates suppressed an inclination to smile at Lindsay's deliberately glassy expression.

'Yes, well, it's good to relax occasionally.'

He leaned forward eagerly across the desk.

'We've made a break-through, Mike. The first real lead we've had in this whole damn business.'

Lindsay eased back in his chair waiting for him to continue.

'The South Australian National Parks and Wildlife people have had a report of a truck picking up a batch of protected fauna in the far north of the State. And when I say a truck I mean a big one, a road train. It was spotted by a cattle-station hand on his way home from a bit of 'roo shooting. It was too dark for him to make a positive identification, but he got close enough to see two men transferring cages full of birds from the back of what looked like an old ice-cream van.'

'When was this?'

'Four days ago, just off the Stuart Highway near Marla Bore. We don't know for sure which way the truck went, but it's ten to one he was heading north, away from the weighbridges and inspectors he would have to go through to the south.'

Coates hesitated as though he expected some reaction from Lindsay.

'It's got to be the pipeline, Mike. There is nothing more inconspicuous on that track than a road train. It's the ideal cover.'

Lindsay nodded. It made sense.

'Luckily we've just got the Fauna Squad established,' Coates continued.

'It's working in close liaison with the State authorities and acting as a central intelligence agency to co-ordinate anti-smuggling operations by the States. There are still major legal problems in prosecuting trappers who move the birds across State boundaries, but at least our fauna people can now follow the operation through from start to finish. It's another source of information for us. It means there are officers out there all the time, moving about the bush, concentrating on tracking down illegal movements.'

Coates paused, wanting to emphasise the importance of his point to Lindsay.

'The Fauna Squad is still in its infancy, but already it is paying off as a valuable and constant form of surveillance within our own department. That's the important thing, Mike. It's our baby. Perhaps it would be more correct to say baby brother. As two investigative branches of Customs and Excise, the Fauna Squad and

Narcotics Bureau will work hand in hand in areas of mutual interest.'

'Does that mean one day I might find myself out in the bush ring-tagging kangaroos?' Lindsay asked.

Coates glanced anxiously at Jamieson. There was no hint of amusement.

'I wouldn't laugh about it if I were you,' Coates warned.

It was a good-humoured rebuke.

'As one of our agents you can be appointed as honorary State ranger,' he added in a mildly threatening tone.

'Right now we've got a parliamentary committee inquiring into fauna trafficking in Australia. It's big business, with enormous profits. I think at this point I'll ask Inspector Jamieson to put you in the picture.'

Jamieson stood up and walked across to a large map of Australia on the wall. He stood to one side of it like a schoolteacher at a blackboard.

'Smuggling into and out of northern Australia is being conducted by well-equipped, highly-organised syndicates using light aircraft, yachts and other small craft to take advantage of the remoteness of the region and its proximity to Indonesia, New Guinea, Timor and Singapore,' he began.

His finger traced the curves of the coastline on the map.

'Between Geraldton on the west coast and Gladstone on the east, there are six thousand miles of isolated, sparsely-populated coastline with totally inadequate surveillance. Even in the high-risk areas you will find one Customs officer expected to control hundreds of thousands of square miles, much of it quite inaccessible by road. We are lucky if these areas are inspected once a year.

'As if that is not bad enough, there are nearly nine hundred airstrips in the north capable of taking light to medium-sized aircraft. Only seventy-five of them are used commercially or are under some official control. The rest are either private or abandoned war-time strips established as part of our northern defence network. In addition, there are literally miles of remote beaches and mud flats suitable for landing light aircraft.

'Quite frankly, the committee is astonished at the ease with which boats and aircraft can enter and depart from these areas of Australia undetected. Foreign fishing boats were observed on rivers miles upstream, and there were many reports of unidentified aircraft flying in from the sea with origin and destination unknown.'

'What about radar, and the defence forces?' asked Lindsay.

Jamieson nodded contemptuously.

'Look, we've got a handful of aircraft and patrol boats to cover thousands of square miles of sea. The patrol boats are flat out chasing Taiwanese fishermen and the R.A.A.F. planes are designed basically for long-range maritime and anti-sub-marine work. Even if they could be diverted to anti-smuggling patrols, they are not really suitable for the job.

'As for radar, well, we've got a radar screen from Darwin Airport but it is no problem for a small plane to slip in under it if it comes in low across the coast.'

'I hope nobody tells the Japs,' said Lindsay.

Jamieson ignored the remark.

'For specific jobs the defence forces co-operate as best they can, but until we get our own aircraft and some more high-speed launches the area is wide open and the smugglers are able to operate at minimal risk.

'And the profits are staggering. We are not talking about an occasional operation but a thriving commercial activity with an annual turnover running into millions of dollars a year.

'Australia's strict controls over the export of fauna

have created a great demand overseas for our unique native species, particularly birds. Conservative estimates of the prices of Australian parrots on the overseas market range from a hundred dollars for a pair of crimson rosellas to three thousand a pair for the rare golden shoulder parrot. A matched breeding pair of golden shoulder parrots can fetch somewhere between eight and ten thousand dollars.

'Most of the birds are so common in Australia that there is no problem catching them. A trapper can net two hundred pairs of Bourke parrots or rosellas in a night at a place like Marla Bore, for example, and sell them, even in Australia, for thirty dollars a pair.'

Jamieson was getting into his stride. It was getting more like a lecture every minute.

'There have been a number of successful prosecutions involving syndicates smuggling Australian fauna to Indonesia and returning with significant quantities of reptiles, monkeys and other species. We have unsubstantiated evidence that back-loadings from Asian centres are also made of illegal immigrants, currency and drugs.'

'You could say that your loss is our gain,' Lindsay interrupted.

Jamieson stared at him silently for a moment.

'I would say it is very much your gain. It's a lot easier to spot a truck carrying a thousand birds than one with a thousand grams of heroin.'

Coates intervened.

'Our liaison man in Kuala Lumpur has passed on a report from Bangkok of regular influxes of Australian birds. At this stage it looks as though a new consignment is arriving every two or three weeks.'

'That fits the pattern of a truck link,' Lindsay agreed.

Jamieson pointed at the centre of the map.

'Marla Bore is just over a hundred miles south of the

Northern Territory border. He could have the birds up at the Top End in three days.'

Coates looked at Lindsay.

'That gives you at least a fortnight before the next lot leaves the country. I want you to get up to Darwin straight away.

'You'll have the full co-operation of the Territory police and fauna people there, but basically you'll be operating alone. They haven't got the manpower to get involved in this until we can come up with something more specific.'

'What about our own man there?'

Coates shook his head. 'We've only got a young administrative officer in the bureau. He is just a liaison link with Customs and the local drug squad. He's got no investigative experience, but he should be useful for local contacts.'

Lindsay stood up and walked across to the map.

'I'll want a light aircraft on standby with a pilot who knows those bush strips,' he told Coates. 'I'll also need a four-wheel-drive vehicle and an undercover girl on the road.'

'Our local inspector would be happy to run you around,' Jamieson volunteered.

I said I want a vehicle not a chauffeur,' Lindsay snapped back. 'An unmarked vehicle. I'm not out checking permits.'

Coates picked up the internal phone and jabbed the button.

'Coates. I want Miss Henderson in my office as soon as she can make it.'

He hung up and turned to Lindsay.

'Have you met her? She's one of our best.'

Lindsay shook his head.

'How old is she?'

'Twenty-six. She'll fit into the scene all right.'

'Well, let's get her on a plane to Adelaide and start her hitching up the road.' Lindsay winked at Coates. 'I want her to become the truckies' best friend, and if she can get a part-time job behind the bar at one of the watering-holes, so much the better.'

Jamieson coughed uncomfortably.

'Well, if I've helped you gentlemen all I can . . .'

'Yes, thank you, Inspector,' Coates cut him short. 'Did you want anything else, Mike?'

Jamieson looked quizzically at Lindsay, then turned towards the door.

'Your people will leave those trappers alone for the time being, won't they?' Lindsay asked. Jamieson nodded.

'How many men have you got in the Darwin area?'

'Only one at the moment, I'm afraid. He is working with the Northern Territory wildlife conservation officers. We are really only just getting established in our own right and I . . .'

'Tell him I'll be in touch when I want him to come and pick up the birds,' Lindsay interrupted.

Coates looked reprovingly at him after Jamieson had gone.

'Really, Mike, you were a bit rough on him. We'll be having a lot of joint operations with the Fauna Squad and we've got to learn to work together. It's just a matter of co-operation.'

'I'll give them all the co-operation in the world, just as long as they do what I tell them and keep out of my way,' Lindsay told him.

He banged his fist on the desk.

'Damn it, Alan. Let's get realistic. When I want uniforms around me I'll call the Boy Scouts. Right now I prefer to deal with these bastards my own way.'

Coates saw the same old hatred flaring in Lindsay's eyes. It had worried him when they were partners in the

31

New South Wales Drug Squad probing the dangerous depths of the Sydney underworld. It worried him now.

'I'd hoped you'd got that chip off your shoulder. It's been four years now, hasn't it?'

Lindsay nodded.

' You don't forget the destruction of a young life, not when you watch it happen and can do nothing about it.' Lindsay paused, distracted momentarily. He quickly shook off the memory. 'Anyway, what are you worried about? It makes me a good agent.'

' You were a good cop before your boy died.'

'We were only busting the small fry. Now we're nailing the bastards who bring the shit into the country. If I was still a family man I'd probably be sitting behind a desk in Russell Street or getting my kicks on an occasional outing with the Vice Squad.'

'Do you see anything of your wife these days?'

Lindsay seemed surprised by the question.

'The divorce went through a couple of years ago. What's the point? We have nothing left anymore.'

He spent a busy few hours at the Woolshed, operating from the office of another agent who was out of town.

He had to disengage himself from the Vasendra case which was no great problem. The affair had reached a natural turning-point. The ship would have sailed for Singapore that morning leaving two of its Chinese crewmen behind to face charges of importation of heroin. Both had claimed independently that their Malay skipper was organising the trafficking, but there was no evidence to hold him and his ship. Lindsay's late-night call, however, had persuaded him to wheeze out the names of his Sydney contacts. It was surprising how quickly that sweating little sailor developed the ability to speak English with his head pressed against the floor and a knife probing his eyeball. The big ex-cop sometimes grew impatient with formality when it came to questioning drug traffickers.

Then he had to study the latest telex messages from Kuala Lumpur, consult the rapidly expanding files on the open-north traffic and organise arrangements in Darwin.

He liked the Henderson girl. She was blonde, sexy and sharp. No red-blooded truckie was going to leave a bird like that standing in the dust. With her police training and four years' experience at undercover work, she knew her business. If there were any hints to be picked up along the road, she wouldn't miss them. Lindsay made it quite clear what was expected of her.

When he took a cab back to his motel, the evening sun was setting on the gentle hills of the Australian capital, bathing the distant mountains in cool, blue shadow. Across the placid surface of Lake Burley Griffin a cloudy column of water rose high above a homing tourist launch while traffic flowed with leisurely ease through lakeside lawns and graceful bridges.

From his tenth-floor room he looked out upon a spacious, beautiful city, its lights already sprinkled like gold dust through the darkness of the trees around Capital Hill. The mirror waters of the man-made lake reflected the glowing illuminations of the buildings, elegant white monuments to the eminence of public service.

He turned from the balcony and opened the suitcase he had flung on to the bed. From beneath the clothes he pulled out a black Smith & Wesson .38-calibre automatic, weighing it thoughtfully in his hand.

Watch your back. In his mind again he heard the parting words of Alan Coates, and his grip tightened instinctively on the automatic.

Yes, this time they were really going to hit where it hurt, cutting the pipeline as it entered Australia, stopping the flow of poison before it reached the cities in the south. This was different from busting small-time smugglers and dopey kid pushers on the streets of Sydney. The closer to the source, the bigger the suppliers and the greater the risks.

He needed no warning. There would be a shotgun riding this one, for sure. Both he and Coates knew that. It was a job for a specialist. Which was precisely why they had given it to Mike Lindsay.

Chapter Three

It was Sydney on the line. He knew it as soon as he picked up the phone and heard the rapid, jarring bleep of the long-distance pips.

'Ray Mead?' It was the same monotone voice. He reached for pen and paper without replying. A pause, then the voice continued: 'What sort of trip did you have?'

'Bumpy as usual,' Mead replied, right on cue. He waited for the message, writing it down as the caller pronounced it slowly and precisely as though carrying out an elocution exercise.

'Powell Creek, 7 December. Freight exchange, 12 noon, 9 December. Buffalo.'

Mead repeated the instructions and the caller hung up without saying another word.

'Friendly bastard,' Mead muttered to himself.

The calls always sent a chill through him. It was like having a conversation with a tape recording. There was no opportunity for discussion. No consultation of latitude in the nomination of dates. To be sure of being at Powell Creek on 7 December to pick up the birds, he would have to leave Adelaide straight away. Luckily he had both trailers fully loaded and ready to go. Sydney wouldn't know about a little thing like that or consider the fact that, if he had to wait for a load, his departure could have been delayed at least a couple of days. He would have looked nice and conspicuous running an empty truck north! The answer was that they didn't give a damn in Sydney. He had to be where they wanted him, when they wanted him, and how he managed it was his problem. He was the transportation expert.

Sue was in the kitchen, sipping coffee and smoking a cigarette over the morning newspaper.

'I've got to be off quick-smart,' he told her.

She looked at him wearily.

'Your case is packed, in the bedroom. I've just got to stock up the fridge.'

He sat down at the table to finish his coffee, watching her delving into the freezer for supermarket packs of meat and frozen vegetables.

It was difficult to imagine how it had been with them. He would get home from a trip and they would make it three or four times that night, starting on the kitchen floor. Now she could do little to arouse him from his tiredness on the few nights they were in bed together. Her figure had gone, despite the constant talk of dieting, and her life was as drab as the dressing-gown she was wearing. He knew she would be back in bed as soon as he left.

They went through the familiar departure routine automatically. There was no need for conversation. She passed the food up to him as he knelt on the driver's seat, packing the items carefully into the refrigerator.

'You will be back by the sixteenth, won't you?' she asked. 'It's Shane's birthday.'

'Carry ample supplies of water, food and petrol. Notify police of your intended destination. If stranded remain with your vehicle. Close all gates.'

The big black and white road sign on the outskirts of town shook with the blast of air from Mead's speeding truck as it left the last comforting cluster of urbanisation.

North of Port Augusta, the dusty southern gateway to the vast emptiness of the Outback, the trans-Australian Stuart Highway became a rough dirt track wandering aimlessly out into the brown desert as though uncertain it would ever find another town.

For a while, as the big truck melted into the shimmering heat haze, Mead could see in his mirrors the familiar pall of white smoke streaming from the power station chimneys. It hung in the cloudless sky like a signal of civilisation over the dirty iron roofs of the little township which straddled the top of the gulf, clinging closely to its shores to gain some relief from the intense heat of the interior.

The bitumen ended abruptly, throwing the truck on to rigid corrugations of dirt and stone which filled the cab with the din and vibration of a pneumatic drill and shook the image of the rapidly receding town finally from the driving mirrors. The sudden, jarring impact tossed cigarette packets and tape cassettes from the windscreen shelf, sent apples and oranges rolling about the floor and jolted open a locker door which swung and banged behind Mead's head. He hung on grimly to the wheel, pulling it into his chest and shouting aloud his abuse of the road as if renewing battle with an old enemy.

For more than two hundred miles the bitumen had given him a smooth ride from Adelaide. Now the narrow hellish track stretched ahead for almost two thousand miles, weaving between dazzling dry salt lakes and dipping repeatedly to cross arid, stony creek beds which could flood so rapidly that a car could be swept away by the rising torrent in the time it took to reach the far side.

At first a single railway line kept company with the road which crossed and re-crossed it repeatedly for no other reason apparently than to ease the monotony of the journey. Mead drove through the S-bends at full speed. There were no crossing-gates, no warning lights, no trains. Every twenty miles or so he passed a line of half a dozen fettlers' huts, deserted by day like some Arab camp, awaiting the sunset when the railwaymen would ride back home along the line on tiny motorised trolleys.

He knew he had to get north as quickly as possible.

Vehicles in the scattered procession coming down the track were heavily caked with thick red mud. It hid the licence plates, blocked out the headlights and was splashed across the windscreen meshes. Even the jerricans and spare wheels chained to the roof racks were spattered with the red stain, making the south-bound cars, with their canvas water-bags hanging from their roof-bars, look more like competitors in a cross-country rally than everyday traffic on a national highway. The drivers waved as they went past in a flurry of stones and fine drifting dust that obliterated the road ahead for long seconds before thinning like a lifting fog as the big truck brushed through it.

More rain was forecast for the Centre, and it was obvious that there had already been some heavy falls somewhere up the track. It didn't take much to cut the road completely. One good downpour could turn the great bulldust holes into deep, clinging bogs which even four-wheel-drive vehicles could not get through. They were bad enough when they were dry, for they were quite capable of dragging a speeding car to a halt in a soft cloud of choking grey dust, but in the wet they could turn a hundred-yard stretch of road into a quicksand littered with vehicles sunk to the axles. Then the only thing to do was wait until it dried out.

When it rained in the north everything stopped. The trucks, the planes, even the solitary passenger train that pottered up and down the fragile line to Alice Springs. Sometimes it stood abandoned for weeks between washaways like a neglected toy after its passengers and crew had been hoisted back to sanity by helicopter.

Mead knew the desert, and the laws of survival. It was to be respected, in the same way as the sea. From the first time he ventured on the road as a company driver, it had fascinated him. It tested a man's skill and endurance, rewarding him with pride. As unpredictable as the sea. Yes, perhaps that was the attraction. He thought of each journey as a voyage with himself as the captain, firmly in command, free to make decisions to cope with changing situations.

He had to stop at Pimba, the first watering-hole, to hook up his second trailer. The transport regulations prohibited linked trailers south of the place so he had to tow them individually over the three hundred miles from Adelaide. It added six hundred miles to the trip in both directions and forced him to leave a loaded trailer and two thousand dollars' worth of linking dolly sitting on the roadside. It was a wonder more stuff wasn't pilfered, even though old Tom Crompton kept an eye on it for him. One day someone would tow the whole damn lot away!

At least this time the trailer was still where he had left it two days before, standing alongside Pimba's solitary building. Like all the watering-holes, Tom's place served as pub, store, post office, petrol station and social centre, for travellers and the surrounding cattle stations alike.

As he swung the truck around in front of the trailer, Mead noted with satisfaction that the old man had already loaded the two drums of aviation fuel. He checked to see they were securely anchored, then tested the tension on the chains holding down the towering load of timber and roofing iron.

He was greasing the turn-table of his dolly when old Tom looked out from the bar and called across to him.

'Ain't you coming in for a coldie, Shorty?'

Mead glaced towards the massive figure blocking the doorway.

'Not this time, Tom. I want to keep moving while the road's still passable.'

Tom affectionately patted the great beer-built stomach sagging over the top of his baggy shorts then returned his right hand to its constant task of wiping the bushflies from his sweaty face.

'There's a bit of mud just north of Kingoonya. You might as well have a couple of drinks and let it dry out.' He jabbed a thumb over his shoulder. 'There's a few of the boys from Woomera in the bar. If we get a tourist bus in it could be a good night.'

Mead grinned. The old man was never backwards in trying to drum up a bit of trade.

'There's more rain on the way, and you know it,' he told him. 'I don't want to be stuck with you for a week.'

He clamped the connecting bar of the eight-wheel dolly to the back of his leading trailer, and climbed back into the cab. He had no intention of getting involved in a drinking session with those rocket range boys. The last time it had gone on until 4 a.m.

'Please yourself,' said Tom, turning to go back inside. 'I hope you get bogged right up to your balls.'

Mead pressed the starter button and leaned out of the window to call out to him.

'Hey, Tom! Are there any inspectors on the road?'

'No. She's all clear. It's getting too hot for the bastards. They won't be back till the end of summer, you see.'

The flyscreen door slammed shut behind his fly-covered back as Mead started to work the truck into position for a link-up. He drove well forward, hands moving in rapid succession round the wheel as though he was hauling in a rope. A couple of truckies came out of the bar and stood watching the manoeuvre with the critical look of professionals. Mead gritted his teeth and felt the sweat running down his chest under his singlet. He stopped when his cab was in the middle of the road and put her into reverse. He could not see the dolly, tucked low behind his leading trailer. The secret was to get a line and go straight back so that the dolly didn't buckle away. Checking those side mirrors was like watching a tennis match. Right! He held her steady and eased her back until he knew the strike plate of the dolly was only a few feet from the rear trailer. Normally he would have jumped out and walked back to make sure it was centred truly as it slid under the tray. Not with these jokers watching! He'd give them something to think about!

The width of the open end of the slot on the turntable gave him precisely twelve inches for error. The truck moved back the final feet in great shuddering jolts to the gasps of the air brakes. Three, two, one foot. He felt her strike, solidly as hitting a wall.

He put his head out the window and stuck up his thumb.

'Right up her in one,' he yelled to the watching pair.

That was class. Sometimes it could take ten minutes of shunting to complete that link-up.

As the two truckies walked away to their own vehicles he reached beneath the steering-wheel to release the load locking lever so that he could edge the prime mover back a few slots under the leading trailer to re-balance as a road train, then, with a 335 h.p. roar from the engine, the whole load moved off in a cloud of dust thrown up by its procession of wheels.

From Pimba the track headed north-west towards the eastern edge of the Great Victoria Desert, littered at first with loose rocks that could smash in the wall of a tyre, then covered by drifts of soft yellow sand blown from the tops of the desert dunes.

41

In eighteen hundred miles there were only four small towns, two of them nothing more than rugged, barren mining settlements, so that a cattle grid or wrecked car by the road, stripped bare to the chassis by a succession of acquisitive drivers, became a significant landmark. A plain steel windmill lifting water from a bore, the only construction in perhaps a hundred miles, drew the gaze of everyone who passed along the track as though it was some architectural masterpiece. So featureless was the country, with its uniform mantle of brown scrub, that the unwary could become hopelessly lost within a few yards of the road if they wandered out of sight of their vehicle.

But there was life all around. Lizards sunning themselves on the bare branches of dead, stunted trees, kangaroos poking their heads up out of the bush, ears pricked, to stare in statuesque concern at the noisy road train as it passed, emus that ran stiff-legged along the track ahead of it sometimes for a mile, too stupid in their panic to veer off into the safety of the scrub. And birds. Thousands and thousands of beautiful birds. Each with a price on its head!

It never failed to amuse Mead as he watched the colourful flocks of parrots and cockatoos scattering in front of his truck that a commodity in such abundant supply could command such staggering prices. It was thanks to more of those ridiculous regulations dreamed up by some desk jockey in a city office who didn't have a clue what it was like out in the bush. He wondered if the bureaucrats knew just how many of their precious birds bounced dead from the front of his truck each trip!

Ah well, it was a crazy world! But at least this particular form of insanity was going to set him up very nicely. If it wasn't illegal, he wouldn't be cashing in on it.

He chuckled to himself as he recalled his reaction that evening five months ago when Collins had told him the rates of pay. 'You'll get five thousand dollars in clean cash for each delivery,' the man had said. Mead almost choked on his beer.

Mead did not have to think too hard about it. After all, he was in the transport business, and he was in it to make a profit. He was not going to turn away the biggest profit of all just because some clown in Canberra or Adelaide had decided it was against the law to move a few birds around.

They were sitting at a table close to the stage at the Capricorn Club with Karen keeping an eye on them as she high-kicked her way through the final dance routine of the night. Mead gave her a wink as Collins left to let her know they were in business.

He couldn't see much risk in it. All he had to do was to meet the trapper at a pre-arranged spot and drop the cages he collected off at the airstrip on the way through to Darwin. It was all done in the isolation of the bush, miles away from the weighbridges, the transport inspectors and the city bureaucrats who said it shouldn't happen.

'You've found us a little gold mine there, baby' he said when Karen returned to their table.

She looked particularly beautiful that night. Her wide blue eyes were bright with excitement as they talked, and he remembered how, when she reached across to take his hand, he felt then, perhaps for the first time, that she really did believe they would make a future together. When the club closed she slipped a light coat over her costume to cover herself for the walk back to her flat. It was a little game she played to please him, to give him something to dream about during the long hours on the road. He loved her in high heels and tights with stage make-up on, just the way he had first seen her dancing in the spotlight. At her flat she gave him his own private show, and he could touch her. When he

43

drew the pins from her blonde hair to let it tumble down her back, she knew the show was over and she took him to her bed.

That night, after he had made the deal with Collins, the love-making was better than ever. It was as though she had accepted his sincerity totally for the first time. She gave herself utterly to him. Already he felt a rich man.

What they didn't know then was that her Mr Collins, the quietly-spoken businessman looking for a discreet transport operator to undertake a regular contract, was in the import as well as the export business.

Mead discovered that the first time he met the plane and the pilot handed him the attaché-cases.

'Collins is waiting for these at the Buffalo Motel,' he explained. 'When you hand them over to him, you'll get your money.'

Collins made no secret about the contents of the cases. He opened them in front of Mead, took out the envelopes and stacked them into a concealed compartment in the bottom of his suitcase. There was a magnum revolver amongst the clothes he tipped out on to the bed.

He gave Mead the empty cases.

'You can give these back to the pilot next time you meet him,' he told him. 'I'm sure you'll want to go on doing business with us.'

Mead smiled to himself as he recalled the remark.

Sure, why shouldn't he want to go on with it? Karen was all in favour of the idea and the prospect of gathering in some quick money was already opening up new horizons for both of them.

Mead's day-dreaming was brought to an abrupt end when he ran into the first mud. It started suddenly with a straight line of dark wetness across the track, and he felt the road train losing traction when the drive wheels

44

began spinning on the greasy surface. He kept an anxious eye on his mirrors as the rear trailer slid out on the bends like a lashing tail.

A long, steady gradient relentlessly wore down his speed. He coaxed the truck on, willing the wheels to give a little more grip. A car was bogged half-way up the slope and he swerved past it without hesitation, ignoring the waves of a young couple standing ankle-deep in mud behind it. If he stopped, he too would be stuck.

The mud ended as suddenly as it had begun. In the fading fiery glow of the sunset he could see the tall dust cloud from another vehicle rising above the horizon some twenty miles away, a hopeful sign that the track was clear ahead.

When he cooked his supper soon after midnight under the sparkling desert canopy of stars, he was almost five hundred miles from Adelaide.

He set his alarm for 5 a.m. and, as daylight came, he was driving through flat, stony country covered by sparse, knee-high scrub. Large stones and bone-shaking ridges of rock across the road forced him to stay in the low gear range. He had planned to clock up a hundred miles before stopping for breakfast but, after he had been on the move for less than an hour, he saw a tyre shredding in his offside mirror, sending writhing strips of black rubber flying into the air and tumbling to the roadside. It turned out he had two wheels to change, for when he checked the others he found another flat on the inside runner of a pair on the nearside. He decided to have breakfast there and then and made himself a mug of coffee to wash away the familiar taste of the vaporous grey dust while he cooked some steak and eggs.

It was 8.30 a.m. and the temperature was just about to pass the century mark as he drove into Coober Pedy's solitary main street, as rough and dusty as the track itself. Most of the homes in the little opal mining settlement were underground, dug deep into the rock to escape the blast furnace heat of the sun.

A group of raggedly dressed Aborigines sitting in the dirt outside the pub waved as the road train went past.

Mead took a quick shower at the service station while the truck was being refuelled. The next town up the track was almost five hundred miles away over some of the toughest stretches of road so it paid to set out from Coober Pedy as fresh as possible.

He was still working his way up through the gears when he saw the girl at the roadside. She was wearing a pair of grubby-looking jeans and an old khaki sun hat tilted back on her head. As the road train approached she got up from her knapsack and held out a board with one word written on it in white chalk: 'Alice'.

His first impression was that she was a foreigner, or at least a stranger on the track. None of the regular girls would have stood on the side she had chosen to hitch. His second was that she had good breasts.

She was smiling up at him. Why not a little company? Habib Khan and his bird nets were right up at Powell Creek, well beyond Alice Springs, so she wouldn't get in the way and it must have been obvious to her they would have to stop for the night somewhere along the road. He took his foot off the throttle. A male, a female and a single bunk was always an interesting combination.

Chapter Four

Mead leaned across to take her knapsack as she pushed it up on to the passenger seat. She hauled herself into the cab with quick agility, giving him a broad smile as she slammed the door shut behind her.

'Wow! Air conditioning! Fantastic!' she gasped, her eyes shining with excitement.

Mead grinned.

'I thought you looked a bit hot out there.'

He began again the long process of working the road train up to its cruising speed, changing gear at first almost with every turn of the wheels on the road.

'What were you doing on that side of the road anyway?' he asked her. 'You would have been buried in dust if I had gone straight past you.'

She looked at him demurely as though hurt that he could even think such a thing.

'I knew you wouldn't do that to me,' she replied. She was mocking him. She had waited on that side of the road deliberately.

He liked the look of her. She was fresh and free, the best sort you could get on the road. They turned up occasionally to add a bit of interest to the endless procession of pros, druggies and decoys with boyfriends hiding behind a rock until the truck pulled up.

He guessed that she was about twenty-four. She was no raving beauty, but when she smiled her whole face lit with youthful enthusiasm that gave the impression right away that she was going to be good company. When she took off the hat her short, curly blonde hair added to her attractiveness. A lot of guys would have put the hard word on her before they let her into their cab, but Mead didn't operate that way. He liked a little uncertainty, a bit of a challenge. He enjoyed working them round to it.

She looked the cab over appreciatively.

'Jesus, what a set-up! You sure believe in travelling in style.'

'This is where I spend most of my life, love,' he told her, pleased that she was impressed. 'You've just stepped into my living room.'

She nodded and leaned forward to switch on the small fan on the dashboard shelf, bathing her face in the stream of cool air as though she was taking a shower.

'Reach your left hand down by your seat there and press the knob you find,' he instructed.

She groped about for a moment and let out a squeal of surprise as compressed air surged into the seat cushion under her. He laughed at her reaction.

'This truck is full of surprises, love. That seat's got a bit of a leak in it so if you feel yourself sinking as we go along just let a little more air in, okay?'

He flicked back the lid of the cassette container.

'If you fancy some music, help yourself. What do you like? Beatles? Stones? Elton John?'

He took a long look at her breasts as she studied the tapes.

'Mine's Ray Mead. What's yours?'

'Jenny.'

'You from Adelaide?'

'No, Sydney.'

She selected the Elton John cassette and handed it to him.

'On holiday?' he asked as he pressed it into the tape deck.

'I suppose you could call it that. I just got fed up with working in an office and thought I'd like to see a bit of Australia. A couple of girlfriends of mine did it a year ago, and they had a ball.'

'And what does the boyfriend think about you going off on your own?'

She glanced at him with a wistful smile.

'He was getting too heavy.' She hesitated. 'There's no way I'm ready to settle down yet to marriage, kids, the whole bit. There's too much to see. I mean like out here it's a different world from Sydney, and most Australians never even get to take a look at it. I mean that's crazy, isn't it? It's all our country and we don't even know it.'

'So where are you going after Alice?'

'Well, I want to get up to Darwin, but I haven't thought much beyond that. I'll have to get a job for a while somewhere anyway to save up a bit more money before I can move on.'

She chattered away cheerfully, pausing only when the truck ran over the rougher stretches of road and the noise of vibration in the cabin forced them to shout to make themselves heard.

'Do you do this run all the time?' she asked. 'Don't you get fed up with it?'

'I like it. You've got freedom out here. There are too many bloody stupid rules and regulations in this business. They try to tell you how long your load should be, how much it should weigh, what weight should be over each wheel, and how many hours you should drive, how many you should rest . . .'

'We're over-governed,' she declared, interrupting him. 'That's what Rick always says.'

An expression of annoyance crossed her face fleetingly. 'That's my boyfriend. He's always saying that Australians are the most over-governed people in the free world.'

'Well, they can stuff their rules. Out here there are no inspectors and no weighbridges. I don't even bother to fill in my log book. Can you imagine any driver on a road like this stopping for what they call their compulsory rest periods when he knows that a few miles ahead of him a creek is filling, or he had just spent most of his allowed driving time changing his wheels? The rules just don't apply out here.'

'Why do they have them, then?'

'Because they're bloody mad bureaucrats.'

'No, tell me really.'

'Because it brings in more revenue for the Government, and makes it tougher for the truckies to compete with the railway.'

She seemed to be thinking that over, assessing it in her mind to decide if she could accept it as a fair statement.

'What have you got on your trailers? I mean what sort of things do you carry?'

'Oh, timber and iron, machine parts, general freight.'

'All going to Darwin?'

Mead nodded, then added as an afterthought: 'I've got to drop off some gear in Alice so I won't be able to take you beyond there.'

She reached into the pocket of the knapsack he had put on the bunk behind her and pulled out a packet of cigarettes.

'How often do you make the trip?' she asked as she offered him one.

He started to feel uncomfortable. This was not the kind of conversation he had in mind.

'You ask a lot of questions,' he said curtly.

'I'm a curious girl, aren't I.' She put it over as a statement of apparent fact, not a question. 'I told you I was out to learn all about Australia.'

'You might learn a lot more than you bargained for out here.'

'Sorry. I didn't mean to hassle you,' she said hastily, raising a hand as if to calm him down. 'Go on, you talk.

Tell me about your mates. You must know them all on the road. How many road trains are there?'

'There you go again.'

'Jesus, forget it!' She took a deep drag at her cigarette. 'Am I allowed to ask how long it will take to get to Alice?'

There was no way he could miss the heavy sarcasm in her voice.

'Listen, love, if you don't like my company you don't have to put up with me for that long,' he snapped. 'I'll drop you off anywhere you say.'

She turned away from him and stared sulkily out of the window at the desolate opal fields, clustered piles of white rock against a flat, brown horizon with clouds of dust floating up from the blowers sucking it out from drill-holes deep below the surface. She reached forward to adjust the fan.

He decided to press home his advantage.

'If you're starting to feel hot, you could take your shirt off. I won't mind.'

'Boy, that's really subtle!' she murmured as if to herself, then lapsed into a long silence.

As the tyres drummed the miles away, the flat, stony country was replaced by soft, shifting yellow sandhills sparsely clad with bare trees from which bird-nests swung like coconuts suspended from the branches. Big balls of dead spinifex bounced across the track in the hot breeze, rolling away across the countryside as though they would travel for ever.

Water was just starting to run in the first creek they crossed, a hundred miles from Coober Pedy. It sprayed out from the wheels when the road train pounded across the primitive rock causeway to lift itself laboriously up the curving track on the far bank.

Mead was becoming increasingly anxious. The worst creeks were still ahead of him and he could see a long line of dark clouds low on the northern horizon. He had little time to spare. If those creeks filled he could be stranded for days.

'I don't like the look of it,' he told the girl. 'Have you noticed there hasn't been any traffic coming south?'

She nodded. 'Do you think the road's cut?'

'Maybe. There's been a lot of rain in the Centre in the last couple of days, and it looks as though there's more to come.'

'They say there's a cyclone heading towards Darwin,' she volunteered.

It was late afternoon when they ran into the rain.

Suddenly it was lashing the front of the truck in blinding sheets and pounding noisily on the cab roof. Mead switched on his headlights and the huge road train lit up like a fairground booth with chains of red and orange light globes glowing along the trailers and across the top of the cab. He craned forward, peering through a stream of water washing down the windscreen too rapidly to be cleared by the racing wipers. Ahead the road was flooded, stretching like a canal between banks built up by highway graders levelling out the ruts and the drifts.

It did not last long. After a few miles the sun was blazing again.

Mead pointed to the road ahead.

'Here comes the reason we haven't seen anything going the other way.'

'Wow! What a crowd!' yelled Jenny. 'Where did they all come from?' She turned round and started rummaging in her knapsack. 'I've got to get a picture of this.'

Mead was bringing the truck to a steady halt.

'This is one of the worst bulldust holes on the road,' he said, indicating the scene in front of them. 'After that rain it will be like a quagmire.'

A muddy tourist coach was slewed across the track,

hopelessly bogged with its rear wheels sunk into the mud up to their axles. It was surrounded by trapped vehicles, tilted and turned at all angles by their final hopeless struggles to escape. There were people everywhere. Some were putting up tents, some were standing in groups just looking at the bog, and others were gathering dead timber from the surrounding bush to spread out on the mud along the pathway they were stepping gingerly across to bring camping gear and food out of the leaning coach.

Two road trains, which had apparently made no attempt to get through, were standing one behind the other in the middle of the track close to the southern edge of the mud-hole. Another road train and a line of cars were waiting on the far side, some two hundred yards away. Cars which had tried to by-pass the bog by driving off the track and beating a way through the scrub were stuck in the bush on both sides.

Mead brought the truck to a halt with its roo-bar a few feet from the back of the rear road train. Before he switched off the engine, Jenny was scrambling excitedly down the side of the truck, having a bit of trouble doing so because of the camera she was holding. Mead stuck his head out of his window and called out to the truckie leaning against the side of the trailer ahead.

'What are you waiting for, Ron? You're blocking the bloody road.'

'We're just admiring the scenery, Shorty,' the other truckie replied. 'It's so nice we've been looking at it for three hours.'

Mead jumped to the ground.

'Nothing wrong with that,' he said, pressing the heel of his boot into the mud.

'No, this is all right. It's the wet bit up there we're worried about.' Ron Beaty inclined his head in the direction of the general chaos.

'Who's up front?'

'Pete Connell. He's over there chatting up the birds.' Beaty indicated a sun-tanned truckie with a group of teenagers setting up folding tables by a couple of gas barbeques.

'Looks as though they are settling in for the week,' Mead remarked drily.

He walked with Beaty along the trailers. The two road trains had been linked together with a straight bar in readiness for an attempt to cross the bog.

'Don't you think you're a bit too old to stand around here perving on the sheilas?' Mead suggested. He slapped Beaty's stomach with the back of his hand. 'With that gut you'd never get inside a sleeping-bag with any of 'em anyway, so why hang about?'

'Well, to tell the truth, Shorty, we were waiting for you to come along and rescue us.'

Mead ignored the remark. He was studying the deep moist ruts in the track, stepping tentatively into them until the thick reddish brown mud oozed over the toe-caps of his boots.

'Just a bit on the greasy side,' he declared. 'We'll get through that all right. I'll link up.'

But Beaty was not going to be rushed.

'We'd better wait until another truck turns up. We'll need as long a spread of traction as we can get.'

'Let's give it an hour and see who comes along,' Mead suggested.

'The boys reckon it's bad up north,' Beaty told him. 'There's water flowing across the road in a couple of places and the bitumen's showing signs of breaking up. If it keeps going the road will be closed north of Alice before we get there.'

Mead's stomach tightened. He pulled the straight bar angrily from beneath the tray of his trailer and carried it up to the front of the truck. He looked around for Jenny and saw her peering curiously into the cab of Beaty's truck.

'Christ, she's a nosy bitch,' he complained to himself.

'Any good?' Beaty asked.

'How the hell would I know? I only picked her up at Coober Pedy. If I can get away from you lot before I make a camp tonight I'll be able to find out.'

'She's not a bad looker. You'd better watch out or young Pete'll latch on to her.'

'I can handle him, and her.' Mead grinned, raising his fist in a phallic gesture. 'She'll be so sore between the legs by the time she gets to Alice she won't be able to walk out of town to hitch the next ride.'

A fourth road train came up from the south while they were drinking their second can of beer. When it was linked to his rear trailer, Mead called out to Jenny, who was in earnest conversation with Beaty.

'Come on. We're going through.'

The long line of four linked road trains moved steadily into the mud with the campers cheering them on from the roadside.

When the engine raced as the wheels started to slip Mead lifted his foot from the throttle and moved up a couple of gears. He could feel the thrust of the rear road train, with its drive wheels still on firm ground, pushing them farther into the bog.

'Keep going, baby. Keep going,' he breathed, willing them through.

'We'll never make it,' said Jenny, perching on the front edge of her seat.

'If we get stuck in this lot we're really in the shit,' he told her.

The front truck was passing the trapped coach when he saw in his offside mirror the back of his rear trailer sliding sideways as the rear truck put pressure on it.

'Left. For Christ's sake keep left,' he shouted as though the leading driver could hear him.

For a moment the whole line seemed about to buckle, then he felt a firm tug on the front of the truck and the trailer straightened out as it took the strain of the weight of the rear unit.

He breathed out in a rush, and glanced across at the girl.

'That was close.' She looked tense, and said nothing.

The campers waved excitedly as the leading truck dragged itself out on to solid ground, keeping going until a foghorn blast from the end of the line signalled that all four road trains were through.

'Does this sort of thing happen often?' Jenny asked.

'Often enough. Once I was bogged with another couple of trucks for five days, and we had to feed all the bloody tourists. I was down to my last can of beans when we finally managed to get through.'

The quick dusk was bringing a welcome coolness as they left the others.

Within an hour they were engulfed in an endless blackness, barely able to see one another in the glow of the control panel. There was only one place to look, down the narrow probe of the headlights bouncing along the monotonous brown track for hour after hour while grey scrub flashed past the side windows with surprising rapidity. In the vastness of the bush night, time and distance were impotent. If there were changes in the countryside, if a landmark had come and gone, they were unseen, out there in the darkness beyond the select reality of the lights.

They felt the weight of solitude compressing their companionship. Mead knew how to use the pressure of the total night. He knew the hypnotic effect of the featureless track and the constant drone of the engine. Despite the bone-shaking corrugations, it had lulled many a driver to sleep at the wheel to wake, if he was lucky, smashing through the mulga with no road in sight.

Jenny was rambling on about her job and her parents and her boyfriend. Mead was on half-listening, putting in a 'yes' and a 'no' occasionally and hoping they fell in line with the general trend of her conversation. He was busy working out the best way to get her into his bunk. In the background he could hear her trying to justify walking out on the bloke back in Sydney.

'Were you living with him?' he asked.

'No, I told you. I had this flat with another girl. That was the trouble. He was living on his own and he wanted me to move in with him. I told him I wouldn't do that unless we were married, and I wasn't going to get married until I'd had a bit more of a look around. I mean travel. You know.'

Mead reached behind him and pulled open the door of the refrigerator.

'Pull out a couple of cans of beer,' he told her. She ripped the tops off them and handed him one.

'It's funny, isn't it?' she continued, ignoring the interruption. 'He's probably the ideal guy for me, the one I should marry, but now I'm leaving him. I suppose by the time I get back he will have forgotten all about me and be hooked on someone else.'

'Probably,' Mead agreed. 'If you were so keen on him why didn't you let him move in with you? Wasn't he any good in bed?'

'Now who's being nosy?' she asked in a disapproving tone.

'Well, don't tell me you weren't sleeping with him. You'll be saying you're a virgin next.'

'I'm not saying I'm a virgin,' she retorted, irritated by his manner.

'Thank Christ for that. I'd never live it down if the

57

boys knew I'd driven a virgin from Coober Pedy to Alice. I never allow them on this truck, or rather I never allow them off it.'

'Well, then, you won't have to bother me, will you?'

'It'll be no bother at all, love,' grinned Mead. 'No bother at all.'

He started telling her about other girls he had picked up along the road, adding a few embellishments as much for his own satisfaction as to impress her. In Mead's version they were all willing and extremely able. He got a kick out of giving her the explicit sexual details.

What was she going to do if she didn't like it? Get out and walk?

She listened mostly in silence, waiting for a chance to get him off the subject with a skilfully placed question.

Mead found himself talking about his marriage. He was not sure how she had managed to sidetrack him on to the topic but she was an encouraging listener and he found that he was glad of the chance to formalise his feelings with words. He told her about Karen and their plans to take a trip to Europe when he finally made the break with Sue.

She was not critical of him, perhaps even a little wary now of stirring his quick temper.

'There's not much of a marriage left to break up when the husband's home only four or five days a month,' she remarked. ' You must have a pretty high divorce rate in your business.'

'Most of the guys are married. Sometimes you'll see them with the missus along for the ride, but mostly they prefer to leave them at home so they don't find out what goes on up the track. A few of them have road wives, girls who live with them while they are on the road. Some of them are real dolls.'

'And what will happen when you take up with Karen?

Won't you still have the same problem, being away from her all the time?'

Mead laughed.

'Look, love, I'm not staying in this driving game for the rest of my life! Before long I'll have my own fleet of trucks running up and down this road, and I won't be one of the jokers driving them. I'll be the boss, roping in the profits. Believe me, Karen's not one of your little women types who will sit quietly at home in Darwin while I'm away down the track somewhere. Once I've got the first few trucks on the road we're off to London, Paris, Rome, the whole works. We're going to live it up.'

It was just after 10 p.m. when he dropped the road train into its low gear range and started to watch the track ahead for a suitable spot to pull off the road.

'I think we'll call it a night,' he told her. 'How do you fancy a nice piece of steak and some new potatoes and maybe some peas or something?'

'Fantastic! I'm absolutely starving!'

While Jenny was still stretching herself luxuriously in the surprising stillness of the bush night, he was collecting timber for their camp-fire. Glad to be on her feet, she ignored the canvas seat he offered her and stood watching the flames snapping the dry wood and filling the air with the sweet smell of burning mulga. The only sounds came from the crackling fire and the road train, clicking and creaking spasmodically as it settled down for the night.

While the fire was building up, Mead made a superficial check of the trailers, walking along them in the darkness testing the tension on the ropes and kicking the outside tyres.

'What's that compartment for?' she asked when he was through, pointing to the store-room for the bird cages he had fitted on the front trailer.

59

'It's a refrigeration unit,' he replied casually. 'For fish, frozen food, that sort of thing.'

She seemed to accept the answer quite happily.

He spread a clean, blue check tablecloth across the breakfast bar and set two places.

'Keep an eye on how that steak's cooking while I open a bottle of wine, there's a good girl.'

'Wine! My, you do live well!' There was that mocking tone in her voice again.

He took a bottle of Riesling from the fridge, nicely chilled. The glasses were plastic admittedly, but she must be gathering by now that he was a cut above the ordinary truckie. As far as he was concerned, it was a foregone conclusion that she would climb into the cot with him. The only thing that worried him was this feeling she was laughing at him. She was an irritating bird.

She didn't say much as they ate. Mead talked most of the time about his adventures on the road while Jenny sipped her wine and watched the trembling mice venture out of the ring of darkness round the fire to steal the scraps of food they threw down.

She didn't want to speak when he stopped talking because she was fascinated by the silence and the stillness of total isolation. It seemed that the bush made a sound of its own, a gentle hum like an open radio channel, so close to the edge of audibility that she could not be sure it was not within her head rather than without.

She stood up and walked out of the firelight, waiting for her eyes to grow accustomed to the moonless night. She looked directly up at a breathtaking ceiling of stars more numerous than she had ever seen before. She rocked back on her heels, almost losing her balance but unable to tear her eyes away from a glimpse of eternity. Under its arch she could sense the roundness of the world, feel it beneath her feet.

'Watch out for Joe Blakes,' Mead called.

'What?' She had forgotten him. She didn't know what he was talking about.

'The Joe Blakes. Snakes,' he explained. 'Just watch out, that's all.'

She stepped cautiously out farther into the darkness.

'And don't let the truck out of your sight. You can get lost in this country just going for a leak. It's a hell of a way to die.'

He was packing away the breakfast bar when she returned to the truck to get her sleeping-bag. He slipped his arms round her from behind, kissing the back of her neck, his hand moving inside her blouse.

She tried to push him away. 'I don't want to,' she said.

'Nobody asked you if you wanted to.' He spun her round violently and gripped her hair, forcing her head back so that she was looking into his eyes. 'You're too good to waste.'

He kissed her forcefully, his hand at the back of her head preventing her from turning her lips away from his. She struggled to break free from him, feeling the roughness of his chin on her cheek and the strength of his body as he pushed her hard back against the truck. He smelt of sweat. She froze.

He stepped back from her angrily.

'I'll give you a couple of minutes to think about it,' he snapped. 'If you don't get your pants off and climb into that bunk you'll walk the rest of the way to Alice Springs.'

She stayed rigid, her head pressed back against the side of the truck while she watched him fearfully. He folded up the chairs and stowed them away in the trailer locker, looking over the ground to see if he had missed anything before kicking sand on to the glowing embers of the fire. Then, as if she was the final thing left to clear up, he turned his attention back to her.

She hadn't moved. He came towards her casually and stood in front of her, laughing at the expression on her face.

'Let me have my sleeping-bag,' she pleaded.

'Look, bitch, you're going to come across one way or the other even if I have to lay you out to get it,' he snarled.

He reached out to undo the buttons on her blouse.

'Let's start right here.' He hooked a finger under the front of her bra and gave it an indicative tug. 'Take it off, then.'

She knocked his hand away and tried to break free from him but he seized her in a pinning grip and forced his mouth down on to hers. She bit his lower lip, making him yell and relax his hold sufficiently for her to shrug herself clear momentarily.

Furious, he caught her wrist with his left hand and swung at her with his right fist. The blow struck her on the temple and she crumpled to the ground. He rolled her over from her side and hit her again across the face with the back of his hand. Wide-eyed with disbelief, she lay looking up at him as he knelt over her.

'Now take that bra off,' he demanded.

Sobbing uncontrollably, her cheeks wet with tears, she struggled to sit upright then reached behind her back to unclip the strap. As Mead stared admiringly at her bared breasts she lay back resignedly on the dirt, her body still shaking with sobs.

'That's better,' he breathed. 'When you're going to be fucked anyway you might as well relax and enjoy it.'

Kneeling astride her, he cupped her ample breasts in his hands and pressed his face between them.

Chapter Five

There was a colourful crowd in the transit hall at Darwin Airport's new international terminal building. It was a typical local mixture; young, cosmopolitan, inelegant.

Many of the men wore nothing more than shorts, rubber foot thongs and sloppy sun-hats. Their women went barefoot in saris and sarongs or long, flowing dresses which clung to their bodies as they moved so that they emphasised rather than concealed their naked-ness beneath. A few, deep-tanned to immunity against the tropical sun, were dressed in brief bikinis while some of the young children ran about completely nude. There were more Asians and Chinese in the crowd than would be found anywhere else in Australia. With the European migrants, standing in little family groups under the swirling ceiling fans, they added half a dozen languages to the general chatter. The most smartly dressed were queueing at the ticket counter to check in their baggage. The rest looked as though they had just wandered in from the beach.

The public address system clicked on and a precisely modulated female voice hushed the hum of conversa-tion.

'T.A.A. announces the arrival of its flight number twenty-four from Adelaide and Alice Springs.'

The crowd started to shuffle towards the full-length windows facing the tarmac. Some teenagers who had been sitting on the floor with their backs against a wall helped each other to their feet and unrolled a welcoming banner.

Mike Lindsay pulled the photograph from his shirt pocket and studied it again. With the others he strolled close to the windows as the high-winged Fokker Friendship turned into its parking position in front of the terminal, the screech of its starboard engine fading into silence with a descending sigh.

He smiled to himself. As an international airport, Darwin had not quite grown up. The new terminal was out of date the moment it was built. It looked modern enough, but as a functional building it had not really advanced the place much beyond the shed-in-a-paddock standard of the country strips. Passengers were still set down on the fierce heat of the tarmac, which came as quite a shock to newcomers stepping into it for the first time from the coolness of a pressurised cabin, and in the torrential afternoon rain of the wet season they had to scurry for the shelter of the terminal through great pools of water. More sophisticated reception arrangements would have made Lindsay's task easier. As it was, he had to jostle with the crowd at the windows to do what everyone else was doing, watching the straggly line of incoming passengers for a familiar face.

He studied them closely as they emerged at the top of the steps at the rear of the aircraft and paused to take a yellow umbrella from the hostess standing just inside the cabin. He dismissed them from his attention one by one as they raised their umbrellas and, crouching under them, hurried down the steps and across the tarmac. Occasionally his gaze flicked to the sheltered doorway of the terminal for a covering check on one of the passengers lowering his umbrella. A momentary glance, and he concentrated once again on the faces still appearing from inside the Fokker.

Ah! There he was! Peter James Burrows, alias Johnny Merchant, alias Richard Jenner, alias whatever name he had chosen for this trip.

So he had changed airlines in Adelaide as well as his clothes! He was wearing a dark brown suit that morning when his Sydney tail saw him off from Mascot Airport. Now here he was relaxed in casual trousers and beach shirt wearing a sporty pair of sunglasses and a camera slung over his shoulder. Lindsay liked that touch. He felt a sudden surge of satisfaction. Peter James Burrows, you are acting in a suspicious manner. The thought delighted him.

The mug-shot did not do Burrows justice. He was a good-looking killer. His fair hair and pale blue eyes made him look to be of German extraction, and he had been out of gaol long enough to have developed a healthy tan. Grievous assault, armed robbery, and a murder charge that did not stick. Lindsay ran through his form in his mind's eye as he assessed him like a race-horse in the saddling enclosure. The Sydney muscle-man moved with athletic ease, stepping out for the terminal with long strides.

He was only a comparatively recent arrival on the Sydney drug scene. If he had appeared earlier Lindsay would certainly have come across him. It was probably just as well that he hadn't, Lindsay thought to himself as Burrows came through the door and walked straight past him. When he did introduce himself he wanted it to be a complete surprise!

He followed him to the laneway at the side of the terminal which served as the baggage collection area and, as Burrows searched the trolleys for his suitcase, he strolled towards the cab rank.

Burrows was among the first out. Ignoring the airline bus, he swung his suitcase easily into the boot of the front taxi and got into the passenger seat. Lindsay made a mental note of the registration number and walked casually towards his car which he had parked opposite the line of cabs. He was right behind Burrows's cab as it waited to turn right into the flow of traffic on the Stuart Highway.

Constant lightning like the flash of a welder's torch lit the heavy dark clouds racing across the city as he tailed the cab along the busy six-lane highway. Through the breaks in the lower layers he could see towering columns of billowing cumulus rising high into the sky, white-topped by the light of the evening sun.

The elevated stilt houses of the Royal Australian Air Force base on his right gave way to more expensive suburban homes set in lush green gardens of fast-growing tropical trees and shrubs. Like most Darwin houses they were perched high on round steel piers or pillars of reinforced concrete to catch the cooling breezes blowing off the Timor Sea. Long and narrow in design so that each room had louvre windows on both sides to make the most of the natural ventilation.

With the long build-up to the wet season already well advanced, the rain fell from the skies in noisy torrents every afternoon soon after 4 p.m., drumming on the iron roofs and slapping against the asbestos walls of the houses as the palms and bougainvillaeas and fragrant frangipanis swayed restlessly in the gardens.

Lindsay had been in the city for little more than a fortnight but even in that time he had noticed a marked rise in the humidity. He doubted that he would ever get used to it. It was like moving about in a hot bath.

The ominous nature of the sky was the first thing that struck him the day he flew in from Canberra. The plane had tilted in great sweeping arcs to weave its way between puffy white pillars of cloud rising thousands of feet above it.

As it swung round one of them, as though invisibly suspended from the top, he looked down through the gaps in the lower layers on the city of Darwin huddled in its isolation between suffocating green jungle and the muddy-edged waters of the sea. It seemed to him then an acutely vulnerable city, absurdly indifferent to the threatening skies rearing above it as if preparing to strike in anger at man's invasion of the wilderness. He recalled that initial impression of menace each afternoon when the rain clouds gathered.

Usually the mounting fury of the sky was spent in a quick, cleansing downpour lashed across the city by the wind while lightning flickered behind the dispersing formations to the thump of thunder, but a few days earlier Darwin had been placed on full alert when a tropical cyclone was reported heading towards it from the Arafura Sea. Remembering his first sight of those skies, he experienced a surprising unadmitted chill of fear. The local radio stations repeatedly broadcast warnings, heralded by an urgent, screeching siren, telling people to batten down their homes and to stay tuned for further instructions.

The alert ended in an anti-climax when Cyclone Selma, as it had been named, veered away from Darwin to pass thirty miles to the north, content merely to fan the city with its hot breath.

Burrows's cab got a green run through the series of traffic lights at the end of the highway where it was intersected by the parallel main streets of the city. Lindsay, who had allowed the gap between them to widen during the six-minute drive from the airport, was now close behind the cab, watching for it to turn left to the city centre. Instead it continued to the Esplanade and then turned into the driveway of the Buffalo Motel, a ten-storey tower which was one of the dominant features of the Darwin skyline.

Lindsay pulled into the same spot in the car park that he had left an hour earlier, muttering to himself about inconsiderate crooks and unnecessary journeys. If he had known Burrows was going to check into the same hotel, he could have stayed in the bar and waited for him to arrive. He accepted the thought philosophically as he headed for the foyer. That was the thing about small towns, he told himself. You were always bumping into people you didn't want to know!

Burrows completed the registration card and the receptionist handed him a key from the rows of pigeon-holes behind her.

'Thank you, Mr Collins. Room six one nine on the sixth floor.'

Lindsay was dialling on the red phone in the reception area as Burrows got into the lift.

'Detective-Sergeant Adams,' he snapped, irritated at the time it took to get an answer.

'Frank? Lindsay here. Our shotgun's arrived. Checked into the Buffalo. Room six one nine.'

Lindsay glanced anxiously back at the lift which had returned to the ground floor with half a dozen passengers.

'Can you get your man down here right away?' He paused, wiping the perspiration from his forehead. 'Thanks, mate. I'll meet him in the foyer.'

He hung up and walked across to the souvenir shop near the hotel entrance.

The young Drug Squad detective Adams sent over was a tough-looking character dressed in a grubby green singlet and shorts so that he looked like a builder's labourer. He leaned lethargically against the reception counter, drinking from a can of beer and trying with little success to chat up the dark-eyed Asian receptionist who obviously viewed him with considerable distaste.

Burrows was back in the foyer within an hour. He threw his key on to the counter and stood waiting just inside the entrance of the hotel until a cab pulled up in the drive-way. Lindsay watched him leave with his scruffy escort in tow, then took the lift to the eighth floor.

He was dozing luxuriously on the bed when the phone rang. It was the young detective. Lindsay looked at his watch. He had been gone twenty minutes.

'He's in a flat in Benson Street,' the cop reported.

'Where's that?'

'Right in the city centre off one of the main shopping streets. Looks as though he'll be here for a while. He's sent the cab away.'

'Stay close,' Lindsay told him.

He took a small, square box from a drawer, slipped it into his pocket and returned to the foyer. The Asian girl was busy at the switchboard, leaving the other receptionist to handle the counter customers.

'Six one nine,' said Lindsay. She ran her hand along the pigeon-holes, reached into one and handed him the key.

Burrows had put his clothes away neatly. Three shirts, a pair of trousers hanging in the wardrobe. Socks, underpants, handkerchiefs in the top drawer of the dressing table. It looked as though he was intending to stay only two or three days. There was nothing out of the ordinary, apart from the total lack of information about the occupier of the toom.

Lindsay lifted the bedside phone and quickly unscrewed the mouthpiece. Taking the small pair of pliers from his pocket, he disconnected the diaphragm and substituted an identical-looking instrument from the box he had brought with him. He replaced the receiver and, after a final quick look round, returned the key to reception and went back to his own room.

He took a transistor radio from the wardrobe and set it up with aerial raised on the writing desk. Switching to the shortwave band, he moved the station selector needle carefully to the left-hand end of the dial. Satisfied, he walked across to his phone and dialled six one nine. He put the receiver down on the top of the bedside locker and went back to the radio, starting to move the needle almost imperceptibly along the dial.

The jarring tones of a ringing phone came over the radio and immediately the cassette tape clicked into movement. Lindsay made a final adjustment then hung up his own phone. As the sound stopped coming over the radio, the tape switched off.

He hummed softly to himself as he slid the radio to the back of the wardrobe shelf. What a pity such a useful gadget was illegal!

Burrows was a real break. After two weeks in Darwin Lindsay had failed to come up with anything concrete. From checks with the freight companies he had compiled a list of thirty road train drivers regularly making the run between Darwin and Adelaide who were open to suspicion. He had passed the names on to Julie Henderson when she had rung him. She was on the road somewhere north of Alice Springs by now, due to make another routine report the next afternoon. So far she had been singularly unsuccessful in spotting anything out of the ordinary.

Lindsay was getting impatient. He knew it would take him weeks to eliminate the drivers one by one from the list, even with Julie's help. The airstrip search had proved equally unrewarding. After an initial aerial survey, he had driven to eleven strips to make a ground inspection without finding any evidence of recent use. The irritating thing was that although he found no tyre marks on the tarmac or heavy vehicle tracks in the bush, he could not positively rule out at least seven of the strips for there were signs of occasional visitors. Cigarette ends, beer cans, campfire ashes. They all looked comparatively recent but were probably left behind by shooters or kids doing a spot of drag racing at the weekends.

The local drug scene was a dead loss, completely amateurish. The supply seemed to be mostly marijuana brought in by young pushers trekking the hippie route from Bali and South-East Asia with a steady back-up of locally grown grass. It was a cool, friendly scene, a daisy-chain of beautiful people. Lindsay would have liked to bang their heads together.

So it seemed the pros were ignoring the potential Darwin market and pushing the stuff straight down south. With the local informants unable to help him and still no lead on the truck, what he needed was a bit of luck. Then along came Burrows.

He had all the qualifications to ride shotgun on the incoming shipments. Lindsay had felt a comforting conviction about that when he got his form and photograph from the New South Wales Drug Squad. The syndicate needed a thoroughly reliable man to oversee the delivery and to keep an eye on its truck-driving courier to make sure he didn't get too greedy. He had to be ready to intervene decisively the moment anything went wrong. Burrows was both ruthless and intelligent. The way he had got off that murder rap had demonstrated that. The Sydney boys were convinced he fitted in somewhere near the top of the local distribution chain and they had only put a tail on him for three days when he packed his bag and headed for the airport. The timing was right. Another big influx of heroin was due. For the first time it seemed to Lindsay that he was getting somewhere.

With a warm feeling of satisfaction and a glow of grateful appreciation for the wonders of science and the voice-activated tape, Lindsay decided to take the rest of the night off. There was a gorgeous blonde dancer down at the Capricorn Club he found very relaxing to watch. He was thinking about her as he took a shower. She seemed to have taken quite a fancy to him the other night, but she was probably just doing her job. You could never tell with night-club dancers.

*   *   *

Ray Mead stood on the edge of a ten-foot-high cliff, staring down at the red muddy waters of a fast-flowing river. Beneath his feet was a broken crust of bitumen. He could see the matching band on the far bank, sitting like a thin layer of black icing on a cake of red-brown earth. The flood had hit the road at right angles and sliced a great chunk out of it as neatly as though it had been struck two deft blows with a mighty axe.

'I've never seen anything like it,' said the perspiring, red-faced little man whose car was the only one on the scene when Mead's truck arrived. 'Suddenly the whole road started moving, and then it was gone. If we had been any closer we would have gone straight over the edge.'

He looked anxiously towards two young children chattering excitedly as they tried to throw stones across the width of the river, and shouted at his wife who was still sitting in the car.

'Get those kids back from there or you'll lose both of them.'

He turned his attention back to Mead.

'How long do you think we'll be stuck here? Could be weeks, couldn't it?'

Mead was deeply wrapped in his own problems. He answered the man irritably.

'Could be a day, could be a week. How the hell would I know? Once the water goes they'll soon put a detour in. There's plenty of highway equipment just up the road at Tennant Creek.'

And just up the road, thought Mead, was old Habib Khan sitting waiting at Powell Creek with sixty cages of birds ready for him to collect. He was less worried about that than about his airstrip rendezvous scheduled for 9 December, just two days away. At least the trapper knew the road and would probably realise the weather had stopped him getting through, but the people in Sydney and Bali were different. They didn't know the country. He had warned them time and again that the road was unreliable, but they would still not let him nominate the rendezvous dates, which was the only sensible way to arrange them. The only concession he had got was a few extra days between pick-ups and the usual inflexible instruction: 'Be there. How you manage it is your problem.'

Well, now it was their bloody problem! There was no way he was going to be able to get through to the strip in time to meet the plane. He was already running behind schedule. It had been a hell of a trip! He had had to use every trick in the book to get through some of those bogs farther south. On top of that he had blown five tyres and lost a battery which had been disintegrated by the vibration. When he got to the start of the bitumen at Alice Springs, just about the half-way mark, he had to spend a whole day repacking his load for fear it would spill from the trailers if it got any more rough treatment.

The only piece of luck he had enjoyed was that Jenny bird. She had turned out to be quite a good lay once she got used to the idea but the silly bitch had refused to talk to him all the way to Alice the next morning. He was glad to see the back of her in the finish.

Two road trains pulled up on the far side of the flood and the drivers got out to stand staring across at them.

'Well, it's no good staying here,' Mead snapped. 'We'd better get back to Wauchope fast before the road gets cut behind us and we're stranded on an island.'

The man took him at his word and headed straight for his car, calling to his two boys as he went.

As the car drove off, Mead disconnected his rear trailer and placed six fluorescent warning cones across the road. With only one trailer he could reverse half a mile to a spot where there was room enough for him to turn round and head back to the Wauchope bar.

Chapter Six

The counter on the tape deck indicated that the machine had been recording.

Lindsay pressed the re-wind button and watched the cassette reels spin briefly. There was a slight pause after he jabbed 'Play' before Burrows's voice came up on the tape. A couple of calls for room service, a reminder from the receptionist that he had not put in his breakfast order. Then a call from outside. Lindsay leaned forward in concentration as he listened to the voice.

'Is that Mr Collins?'

'Right.'

'There's no way I'm going to make it on time. It's impossible. The road's cut, washed away completely. It could be days before it's open again. Nothing can move north . . .'

Burrows interrupted him.

'Have you made the first pick-up yet?'

'No. Haven't got that far yet.'

'Right. Call in as soon as you can but do not collect this time. Cancel all arrangements for this trip. Cancel everything, proceed with your normal run. Understand?'

'Okay.'

'You will be contacted in the normal way.'

'Okay. I'm sorry about this. There's nothing I can do about it.'

Burrows hung up, the sound of the phone being replaced amplified out of proportion by the microphone in the mouthpiece. Lindsay let the tape run silently for a while before switching back to the start and listening intently again to the whole conversation.

The call had come in within the last three hours, for the receptionist's reminder was the last thing on the tape when he had checked it that morning.

Lindsay took a map of the Northern Territory from a drawer and studied it as he considered the situation. The aircraft must be due at any time now, certainly within the next forty-eight hours. Burrows might cancel it but it was more likely that he would meet the plane himself rather than run the risk of having a major drug consignment held up somewhere in the pipeline. As shotgun for the delivery he would have gone to the airstrip in any event to watch the pick-up from a concealed viewpoint and tail the truck into Darwin to ensure that nothing went amiss and instructions were obeyed to the letter.

That truckie didn't realise how lucky he was being stuck on the road. By missing the rendezvous he was going to miss being arrested. It was irritating, but Lindsay had no choice. Burrows would lead him to the airstrip and as the drugs were being handed over he would step in and nail both Burrows and the pilot.

Judging from the reference to the first pick-up, the truck had not even reached the trappers, and with no birds on board it was as clean as any other vehicle on the road. There was nothing Lindsay could do about that, and he certainly wasn't proposing to stand back and allow a load of drugs to be brought into the country just because the Fauna Squad was missing out on its side of the action.

Lindsay looked at his watch. It was just after 2.00 p.m. He made a few quick telephone calls.

The road was cut in two places in the Northern Territory—just south of Tennant Creek and at the Finke River crossing one hundred miles north of the State border. The South Australian section was also rated as generally impassable.

'The road's cut, washed away completely,' the voice on the phone had said.

The choice of words seemed to eliminate the Finke River as the place where the truck was stopped. It didn't sound like a truckie's description of a flooded creek crossing. The truck could still be in South Australia but, if his theory about the plane's arrival being imminent was right, Lindsay had to assume it was farther north, which would place it just below Tennant Creek. Julie Henderson was due to call him at 4 p.m. With a bit of luck she could be in that area.

Frank Adams responded enthusiastically to Lindsay's request for two plainclothes officers to be on stand-by with a car.

'I'll come myself,' Adams told him. 'I don't want to miss out on this one.'

Lindsay was working on his report for Canberra when Julie's call came through. She was at Elliott, one hundred and sixty miles north of Tennant Creek, still with nothing solid to report.

'Don't worry,' he told her. 'I think our man is getting close to you. What's the weather like? Is traffic moving on the road?'

'Sure. It's hot and dry here and there's no problems but they reckon the Stuart Highway's cut down at Tennant Creek.'

'That's where I think the truck is. I've asked Tennant Creek to compile a list of all the northbound trucks stuck at the washway and I'll let you know the interesting ones before they get to you.'

He pulled a list of names from the drawer.

'You can cross off Williams and Morelli,' he told her. 'They both check out clean.'

'Right, Mike. Do you want me to move down to Tennant Creek?'

'No, stop where you are. You won't be able to do

much looking for him across a washaway and once he gets on the move again he is unlikely to stop at Tennant Creek. There's more chance he'll call in where you are.'

Julie sounded doubtful.

'Is that likely if he's got the birds on board?'

'He won't have them on board. He's missed out for this trip so he should be fairly relaxed. He'll probably enjoy a bit of female company.'

'Most of them do. I've got paw marks all over me.'

'It's all in a good cause,' Lindsay grinned, an image of Julie's trim figure flashing into his mind. 'Think of it as a fingerprinting exercise.'

'They never taught me this method at the academy.'

'It can only be learnt in the field. I'm sure you'll make out.'

'Right you are. I'll get back to you in forty-eight hours unless I have something sooner.'

'One other thing, Julie. The trappers could be somewhere near you too, so keep those pretty eyes skinned.'

Lindsay hung up and looked again at his map. Which airstrip? Burrows would show him. Now it was just a matter of waiting until he made his move.

The move came at 3.30 a.m. when Lindsay was snoring peacefully in his motel room. Two floors below Burrows's alarm clock rang briefly awakening him to the sound of rain washing against the windows.

The young cop sitting in his car at the front of the motel had positioned it so that he had a clear view of the foyer entrance and the reception desk. The night manager was engrossed in his novel. He had not moved for an hour since the last late arrival had picked up his key. The rain was drumming the roof of the car, drowning out the sound of the radio which the detective had been using to keep himself awake. He could not see the dark figure walking silently away from the fire-escape door on the far side of the building.

Burrows did not know he was there. He was going through his standard routine. He assumed at all such times that he was under observation, and acted accordingly.

He went out through a gate at the back of the block which led to the car park of the next motel. Moving quickly along the vehicles, he checked the doors. The fifth one he tried opened and he slipped into the driver's seat, throwing his suitcase into the back. It was a late model Holden sedan, manual transmission. Suitably fast and inconspicuous for his purpose, he thought. He took a cluster of keys from his pocket and fired the motor on the third try.

As the first light of day silhouetted the jungle sky-line, Burrows was driving south along the Stuart Highway, the water on the road hissing under his wheels and rising behind him in a sudden mist. This was the coolest hour but, although the rain had stopped, the air was full of moisture as the hot, scented breath of the bush surrounded him in a physical embrace. Burrows savoured the smell and the feel of it. It reminded him of Vietnam. He was never afraid alone in the jungle, for he became part of it. It was when he was in company that he felt vulnerable, like on those stumbling patrols that invited death from the under-growth. So he would slip away when he could to immerse himself in the savagery, to become the deadly part that was feared, to hunt his enemy safely alone with the silent edge of a knife.

He had the same feeling of self-security now. At any time in the human haze of Sydney, or even in Darwin, he could be watched and approached unexpectedly, a hand laid on the arm the signal that the trap had already closed. Here he was alone again with the protective wrap of space around him. In the darkness he had pulled quickly off the road into the cover of the bush to satisfy himself finally that he was not being followed. Now anyone approaching him would be seen and in danger.

He had taken his time on the road so that there was sufficient daylight for him to find his way through the bush to the airstrip without having to use his headlights. He passed the hill where on previous occasions he had watched through binoculars as Mead had loaded his cages into the plane, and drove out on to the runway.

As he turned the car into the trees at the end of the strip he wished he had brought some food with him. He was hungry already, and the plane was not due until midday. It would just about be leaving Bali for Kupang where it had to make a refuelling stop. Burrows got out of the car and stretched, looking around at the busy morning air, relaxed almost now but still instinctively alert for any sound beyond the echoing chorus of the jungle birds. Drawing confidence from his solitude, he lifted the suitcase from the back seat and draped his large frame as comfortably as he could across it to settle in for the long wait.

The plane was fifteen minutes early. As it approached Burrows hurriedly tipped out the contents of the suitcase and carried it out on to the strip. Using a penknife he lifted the false bottom and took out a sheet of bright yellow plastic which he unfolded on the tarmac. The plane made one low pass then banked away into its landing circuit.

'What happened to the truck?' the pilot asked.

'It's stuck down south somewhere. The road's cut. Let's have those cases.'

The pilot was already opening the wing locker.

'Yes, he was worried about the weather last time.'

Burrows was rapidly lifting transparent packets of cannabis and hashish from the attaché-cases and packing them tightly into the bottom of the suitcase. The heroin

was in sealed brown envelopes. There were two kilo-
grams of the stuff, bought by the syndicate for three
dollars a gram in Bangkok and worth a cool million on
the streets of Sydney.

'Will you have any problems about refuelling?'
Burrows asked.

'No worries. I'll keep under the radar until I'm out of
range then I'll turn round and make a conventional
approach to land at Darwin Airport. With no birds on
board there's no reason why I shouldn't drop in there to
refuel.'

Burrows emptied the last case and snapped the locks
shut. He handed it back to the pilot.

'Well, that's it. You can tell our bloke in Bali the next
consignment will be in a fortnight's time. We'll confirm
as usual by phone.'

'That makes it about Christmas.'

'So what?' snapped Burrows. 'We don't take public
holidays in this business.'

The pilot shrugged and pressed down the lid of the
wing locker. He hesitated.

'Did you camp out here overnight?' he asked,
uncertain of his ground.

'No, why?' Burrows was irritably fingering the large
green ring on his left hand.

'Well, someone did. There's a tent down the far end of
the strip. Over on the other side up on a ridge.'

Burrows reacted as though a sniper's bullet had
brushed his ear. He spun the man round and pushed
him roughly towards the plane.

'Move! Go, you bloody fool! Why the hell didn't you
tell me before?'

He was in the car and speeding down the strip before
the aircraft had started to taxi for its take-off position.

As he neared the end, Burrows spotted the small,
green tent amongst the trees on the hillside. From that

position an observer had a clear view of the entire runway, although the tent itself was difficult to see from below. A man, naked but for a pair of shorts, was scrambling up the hill and then running along the ridge, jumping and stumbling over rocks and fallen timber. He was holding something in his hand Burrows saw as he turned on to a narrow track at the end of the bitumen. Binoculars! The man disappeared over the far side of the ridge.

Burrows gripped the shuddering steering-wheel grimly as the car pounded the rocky path, showering stones into the bush when it slid round the curve at the foot of the hill. He braked violently as the track took a suddenly twisting turn to the left then forked at a clearing in the trees. Accelerating, he clung to the right-hand track which was taking him round behind the hill.

A battered blue utility was racing off in the direction of the main highway. Burrows cursed and turned after it. His 357 magnum was among the suitcase contents on the rear seat under the case itself which he had hurriedly thrown in when he left the plane. There was no hope of reaching the revolver while he was on the move. He couldn't see the other vehicle for the dust it raised. He gritted his teeth and kept the throttle open as he went through a sharp S-bend. Coming out of it the car's tail slid sideways, smashing against a tree with a solid thump. Burrows changed down and wrenched the car back on to the track, angry at losing precious seconds.

Suddenly he was looking down on the black ribbon of the highway. The blue ute was just turning on to it in the direction of Darwin, leaving the dust cloud behind at the road's edge.

Burrows knew he had about sixteen miles of winding road in which to catch him before he reached the

Adelaide River settlement. The ute looked well past its prime. He should be able to overhaul it in that distance.

The rattling din of stones flung against the underside of the car ended abruptly when he drove on to the bitumen, the speedometer needle moving steadily round the dial as he kept the accelerator pedal pressed flat to the floor. He soon had the ute in sight and relentlessly closed the gap between them. It was doing just over 80 m.p.h. and Burrows doubted that the driver could get another yard out of it.

The road went down a long decline and Burrows was right on his tail as they blazed into a right-hand turn. A road train appeared with nightmare suddenness from the opposite direction and he saw the ute's worn tyres drift across the smooth surface as it swerved to avoid it. Burrows felt the punch of fear in his guts as he desperately struggled to keep the car on the road and the great truck went past with a roar. He accelerated and his nearside wheels came back off the dirt.

That had been close.

On the straight stretch the ute edged from one side to the other to keep him behind it. Another truck was coming south. The ute driver waved frantically from his window as it approached, and the truckie blasted his horn.

A road sign warning of twisting road ahead. The ute took the first right bend with the car pressing it hard. As it came back for the left turn Burrows saw his chance. With screeching tyres he got the nose of his car into the space on the nearside of the ute. He was alongside it in a second as he cut across the bend, hearing the violent scrape of metal as the ute's front fender gouged the side of the car. With no road left for it the ute plunged over the shoulder, flattening bushes and bouncing off a solid eucalypt to crunch to a halt on its side at the base of an ant's nest. The wheels were still spinning when

83

Burrows reached it, and the only other movement was the drip of water from the shattered radiator.

The driver's face was too mangled to tell his age. His legs were crushed in the wreckage of the cabin. Burrows lifted open the passenger door and reached inside. The mess was still breathing. He walked back to his own car and took the hydraulic jack from the boot.

It was awkward in the confined space. There was no room to swing the jack. He smashed it down on the driver's head as though he was rubber-stamping a document. Three times before he was satisfied the skull had caved. After a brief search he found the binoculars and took them with him.

He drove back to the airstrip to get rid of the tent. There was not a lot to dispose of—a blanket, some clothing, a transistor radio, a haversack with food and cooking utensils, a .22 rifle and some packets of shells.

Burrows fingered through a wallet and pulled out a driving licence. Ian Markham. Date of birth: 18/9/1952. Brisbane address. He noted that with some satisfaction. The ute had been registered in the Northern Territory. Probably working in the area and taking time off to do a spot of shooting, Burrows thought to himself as he packed up the tent.

He carried all the gear down the hill and put it into the boot of the car. What he could not burn would have to be split up and hidden at various points along the road.

Within half an hour of returning to the tent he was back on the highway, heading south. It was 2.30 p.m. He still had time to catch the late afternoon flight out of Katherine.

Chapter Seven

It was bad enough he had to report to Canberra that Burrows had given him the slip, but what made it worse for Lindsay was the certainty in his mind that another major consignment of drugs had just been smuggled into the country under his nose while he stood back sniffing the air like a blind dog. It was probably already in Sydney. For sure there would be heroin in it, heroin that the dealers would cut down to three per cent pure and the pushers on the streets mix with flour, strychnine and cement as they grabbed more powder for themselves. And somewhere excessive greed would create the lethal dose that would kill some stupid kid within seconds of easing the needle into his flesh. Just like Paul.

Lindsay's big hand tightened round the glass of beer as if to shatter it as his face contorted with inner pain. The low growl sounding in his throat was choked off before it became a scream of rage. The man next to him at the bar turned to look curiously over his shoulder.

Lindsay gulped down his beer and brought himself under control. After all it was four years ago, he thought, and immediately reprimanded himself for suggesting that time should make any difference to his feelings of outrage and sorrow at the needless death of his son. The marriage was breaking up anyway. It was doomed long before Paul died and its only visible bond removed. It was doomed long before Lindsay stayed out every night to hunt the streets of Sydney.

If only she hadn't said it in one of those last awful

fights when they clawed at one another as they were torn apart. 'It's no good going out there to look for the killer.' She was screaming as he opened the door, jabbing her finger at him like a madwoman. 'You're the killer! You're the killer!'

It was not true. But how could she even think it?

Someone slapped him on the shoulder.

'Mike! Just in time for your round, I see!'

Lindsay liked Frank Adams. He had not met him before he came to Darwin, but the local cop had accepted him with the typical warm friendship of the Territorians. The informality, the easy-paced atmosphere of a tropical city had been a great help, the co-operation of the Territory police first rate. There had not been the suspicion or resentment at the intrusion of a 'Canberra' man he had experienced elsewhere. He wandered freely about the station, strolling into the offices of senior officers, helping himself to files, using the phones as though he was part of the force establishment. Even his 'official inquiries' at the freight company offices tended to develop into matey chats. As soon as Lindsay had introduced himself, the local manager, almost without exception, would pull a couple of cans of beer from his office fridge as though they were an essential part of any serious business discussion. It was always too damned hot to refuse. Darwin people boasted that they drank more beer per head than any other Australians, and he had no reason to doubt them.

Lindsay grinned at Adams.

'What are you having?'

'Beer.'

It was just after 10 a.m. and there was a big, noisy crowd in the Hot-n-Cold bar of the rambling Hotel Darwin. A group of hippies was monopolising the pool tables in the far corner and a cheer went up as one of the players, wearing one of the popular floral Balinese shirts, potted the black. His long, dark hair was pinned by a headband to prevent it falling across his face as he played his shot.

Lindsay nodded towards the suntans and sarongs.

'I reckon I could pick a Darwin bird at two hundred paces in Sydney,' he told Adams as he pushed a beer towards him. 'Bare feet and bare boobs. You can't miss 'em. Especially the way they move.'

'They're not really our birds, you know,' Adams replied. 'They come and go. We're just a staging-post for the beautiful people moving up and down the road to Asia and Europe.'

He nodded towards the group at the pool tables.

'We had six hundred of them camping just down the road on Lameroo Beach until February this year when the council decided to clean them out and rip down their tree houses. The hippies coming down the route would arrive in Darwin asking for the Royal Beach Hotel. That was the name they had for it all the way from here to London. The locals called it Happy Beach. The hippies would wander in from Bali with a bit of pot or some acid, and know that they'd have no trouble finding somewhere to sleep. Since they got turfed off the beach they've spread out into pads all over town. Some places have up to thirty people living in them, kids and all, in utter filth.'

'Maybe it wasn't such a good idea to kick them out from Lameroo,' Lindsay suggested. Adams nodded.

'At least then we knew where they were. It's the poor, helpless kids that get me.'

'I'll kill that bastard next time,' Lindsay snapped. 'Never mind about a neatly sewn-up arrest with the stuff in his hands. I'll blast a hole in his head and ram some of the shit into it so it'll come out of his ears for evidence.'

'Relax, Mike. You know it's not the first time a tail has been flipped.'

'It doesn't make it feel any better.'

'Just cool it, for Christ's sake. You would have been bloody lucky to nail him the first time after you got here. You didn't have the contact point, the time or even the date. You had no chance of staking it out, and I can assure you that even if you had seen Burrows slip away from the motel you had little hope of tailing him at night on these roads without him knowing.'

Lindsay looked at him thoughtfully. Perhaps he had built up his hopes beyond reasonable expectations. Perhaps he was over-reacting because his pride had suffered, because he had been deprived of the anticipated gratification of pulling off a major coup within a fortnight of starting virtually from scratch.

'If I could go back forty-eight hours, I still wouldn't bring the reception desk into it,' he said quietly.

Adams smiled. He had not seen decisive Mike Lindsay indulge in uncertainty before.

'Sure, it was the right decision. Burrows is a pro. He would have sensed the attention. And this is a small town. There's no point in spreading your business around. As it turns out, it would probably have made no difference if you had asked to be notified when he was leaving. You know how it goes.'

With a wink, Adams played the charade, approaching the bar as though it was the motel reception desk.

'Good evening. Look I won't be leaving until the morning but I'd like to settle my account now if you don't mind. Nice to know how much you have to spend on your last night in town. No, I won't be ordering any breakfast.'

'God, you'd make a hopeless con-man,' Lindsay told him good humouredly.

'The point is, Mike, that at least we can be reason-

88

ably sure he didn't know we were on to him. He was just going through routine precautions, and he thinks he's got away with it.'

'He's not bloody well wrong either,' Lindsay snorted.

'Then they'll stick to the same routine, and by next time we should be ready to grab the lot of them.'

'I hope you're right. Has that stolen car turned up yet?'

Adams shook his head.

'I checked through the day book before coming over here. Things are pretty quiet. A break at the Nightcliff shopping centre, a couple of drunk drivers, a fatal down at Adelaide River.'

'My money says it was Burrows who took it. Too neat a coincidence for him and a car to disappear from neighbouring motels on the same night.'

'Looks that way,' Adams agreed.

He put a two-dollar note on the bar and tried to catch the barmaid's eye. Lindsay lapsed into a thoughtful silence, abstractedly prodding an empty cigarette packet on the floor with the toe of his shoe. Adams searched for something to say.

'The fatal was interesting. Young bloke working for a local builder. He'd gone off on his own to do a bit of camping and shooting but there was nothing in the vehicle when it was found. He didn't even have any money on him!'

Lindsay didn't seem to be taking much notice, but Adams kept on talking.

'It looks as though there was a bit of skylarking going on when he ran off the bitumen. A truckie reported in at Katherine and reckoned he was nearly driven off the road by a couple of idiots having a race up the highway. The other driver must have got scared because he hasn't shown. It was another truckie that reported the wreck.'

Lindsay looked up at him.

'What colour was the other car?'

'Don't know. The kid was in a ute.'

'Was there an airstrip nearby?'

The cop's eyes widened.

'Hey, come on! You don't think . . .'

Lindsay picked up the two dollars from the bar, grabbed Adams's wrist and slapped the note back in his hand.

'Let's go and find out!'

They crossed the street to the police station, a modern, concrete building set back off Mitchell Street behind its own service road. The operations sergeant in the radio room upstairs beckoned as they walked through the door.

'The D.I. was looking for you about ten minutes ago, Frank,' he called.

'Okay,' Adams replied. 'Tell me. That fatal at Adelaide River yesterday. Did the truckie give a description of the other vehicle?'

The sergeant turned back the pages of the day book, running his forefinger quickly down the entries.

'I remember it came in before the accident report,' he said. 'Ah, here it is. It was 7.05 p.m.'

He studied the entry momentarily and turned the book towards Adams and Lindsay.

'No, nothing there but the log of a complaint passed on by Katherine. Vehicles travelling north. Traffic would have more details. They've got the docket.'

Lindsay gripped Adams's arm when they were back in the corridor.

'Why don't you go and see what D.I. wants while I have a chat with Traffic?' he suggested. 'I'll meet you in your office.'

Lindsay was pouring over a government survey map when Adams returned.

'The car's been found,' Adams told him. 'The one Burrows took off in. It was tucked away in a back street in Katherine with a nice scrape down the offside.'

'It figures,' Lindsay responded, still intent on the map. 'That explains why Burrows stood me up at Darwin Airport last night.'

'And what did you find out?'

Lindsay looked at him with a gleam of conviction in his eye.

'Well, let's put it this way. I think it's about time homicide started taking an interest in the road toll.'

The wrecked ute had been lifted back on to its wheels, probably to facilitate the removal of Markham's broken body, and the driver's door ripped off. Like a severed limb, it lay on the ground a few feet away from the wreck next to a tall ant hill. Someone had already removed the battery, the distributor and plug leads, leaving the bonnet raised for the next passer-by who felt like collecting a few spares. Lindsay was surprised the wheels were still on the chassis. There was no need to tow away a wreck in this country. Within a few hours the motoring vultures would pick it clean of every detachable part, leaving a rusting skeleton to be swiftly interred by the gentle embrace of the undergrowth.

Lindsay searched the inside of the vehicle with careful thoroughness. The steering-wheel was broken and there were blood-stains on the dashboard and the floor beneath the shattered windscreen. He turned his attention to the dented, crumpled exterior of the ute, bending down in front of it to run his finger along the top of the nearside end of the bumper bar. He studied with satisfaction the minute flakes of fawn-coloured paint that clung to the sweat on his skin.

'Stolen vehicle: 1973 Holden Kingswood sedan, colour fawn, registration number NES 748. Taken from car park of Koala Motel between 12.30 a.m. and 7.45 a.m. 9 December.'

With their usual persistence the bushflies were trying to crawl into his eyes and mouth. He kept his lips tightly closed, waving a hand across his face in a futile attempt to drive them away for they refused to budge until they were brushed from the skin. He combed the ground around the wreck in an expanding circle until he was convinced that there was nothing of significance for him to find, then returned to the road and walked slowly southwards along the bitumen, stopping to squat and study some skid marks where it swept round the corner.

The frustration of letting Burrows slip through his fingers was forgotten as he drove steadily towards Katherine. He was tensely excited, watching eagerly the right-hand side of the road for any sign of a track into the bush. The strip could not be far away now. According to the map, it was within twenty miles of Adelaide River.

The first thing he saw was the stones sprayed across the road. He had to swing the Range Rover to the left to make the sweeping turn on to the track. In the driving mirror he could see the highway dropping away below him as he climbed through the trees. The track seemed disturbingly narrow at first, but at the top of the rise it widened and his confidence surged back when he saw the old, broken bitumen. The bush ahead was still thick, with no sign of a break in the trees. A lizard hurried laboriously across the track, now rough and stony again as it went into a sharp bend. A splintered tree on the right-hand edge caught Lindsay's eye. He stopped and got out to examine it. From the foot of the scarred trunk he picked up the broken red remains of a tail light, slipping them carefully into his shirt pocket.

He was hurrying now, anxious to dispense with the last lingering reserve of uncertainty.

Quite suddenly there was a clearing in the trees ahead and he drove out into open sunshine. He stopped the Range Rover and sat staring for a while as though in disbelief at the long airstrip shimmering in the afternoon heat with hawks hovering above it on the rising currents of air. It seemed too big, too obvious to be a secret place. He raised both hands from the wheel as if to greet it, continuing the movement to end up with palms pressed against his temples as he leaned back to suck in a deep breath of relief.

There were the black stains of aircraft tyres on the end of the runway. Lindsay drove down the strip, turning off to check each taxi-way leading into the trees.

At the far end of the strip, close to the fringe of the jungle, was a group of large concrete slabs. He could see a black patch on one of them where a fire had burned. The ashes must have been swept away, or perhaps washed off by the rain. He walked round the edge of the concrete, studying the ground closely. On one side he found some charred pieces of timber, then a different blackened object caught his eye. He prodded it at first with his foot, shaking the ash from it, and slowly bent down to pick it up. A broad smile crossed his face. In his hands he held the burnt but clearly recognisable remains of a large bird.

Chapter Eight

Like some strange pagan priest making a ritual offering to the setting sun, old Habib Khan stretched his hands skywards, opening them to release a squawking parakeet which flew off towards the distant lake with a flash of red, yellow and blue plumage.

He swung open the door of another cage, reaching inside with a great, leathery hand to sweep out a spray of excited finches which fluttered about his head uncertainly while he waved them away good-naturedly as if they were flies.

'Buggers don't wanna go, Ray,' he smiled. 'First don't wanna go in the cages, then don't wanna come out of 'em.'

Ray Mead leaned back against the side of his truck, watching him taking the cages from the back door of his old ice-cream van and piling them empty on top of one another as he released the birds. Flocks of water-fowl skimmed across the rosy surface of the lake, settling and rising again in a constantly-changing pattern of black specks.

'Those are dollar notes flying away,' Mead said moodily.

The old man straightened up and looked at him, pushing the brim of his sweat-stained bush hat up from his forehead. His face was brown like the desert dust.

'That's your trouble, you know. You gotta see everything as money.'

He held out a wide-eyed bird, its brilliant red head and deep blue tail feathers protruding from his gentle fist.

' 'Ere, try cashing this one at bank. It's a bird, boy.

Just a bird. Millions of 'em flying about this country and they ain't worth a damn thing, 'cept to other birds, I s'pose.'

'You're a silly old fool. If you had any sense you'd give up trying to think.'

'Me not the fool! The fool he's the joker sitting back in town somewhere telling me I can't have this what I've got in me 'and! He's the fool, no worries.'

Mead ground his cigarette into the dust and began walking along the trailers to check his tyres. He tended to treat old Happy as a bit of an idiot. It was difficult to take him seriously listening to typical Australian phrases distorted by that indefinable accent of his. His father was Afghan, his mother Irish, and he had lived in Australia since he worked as a boy driving camel trains with supplies for the cattle stations up the Strzelecki Track.

He followed Mead along the road train, still holding the crimson rosella.

'Ten dollars a pair I gets for some of 'em. So 'ow much does he get when he can fly 'em out the country? It's crazy, crazy. It's just like when I was 'roo shooting. One days they's paying you to shoot 'em and next they tells you it's illegal and you's out of work. Bloody bastards!'

'You just don't like them because they can read and write.'

'Yes, what do they do with it? Me tell you this. They take old ladies' pet parrots out of their cages and sell 'em to make money for the bloody Government. Don't let 'em go. No! Sell 'em to dealers 'cause they've give 'em a bit of paper to say it's okay for them to keep birds. You understand it?'

'I understand we've lost a packet now the plane's gone without them,' Mead snapped. 'Why don't you run them down the track and sell them to one of the local dealers?'

96

'Too risky, boy. In couple weeks I pick up me money in Darwin so why I want to go south? And some of 'em are dead already, look. They don't last long in them cages. No worries, next time you come I put up nets and have hundreds for your aeroplane. Making more money here than when I was digging opal.'

Mead took some cardboard cartons from a trailer locker.

'Here's your beer and cigarettes, you old bastard. Make sure you keep away from the pub or you'll talk yourself into gaol.'

The old man slid the packages into the back of his van.

'You want to stay for a meal?' he asked. 'Got some good rabbit tonight.'

'No, I'm calling in down the road for some decent tucker.'

'More like you be after one of them whores.'

'At least I don't fuck blacks,' said Mead.

There were two mud-spattered trucks and a few tourist cars parked outside the Elliott bar. It was a primitive little building made from stone, timber and fibreboard with a cluster of outhouses gathered close to its iron roof, and a dirty, ancient petrol pump standing in front of it.

In less isolated circumstances it would have been a place to ignore, to drive past without a second glance with sure confidence that something more auspicious would be found up the road. But here, in the remoteness of the Northern Territory bush, Elliott was an oasis, the only building in more than two hundred miles of relentless road across flat, featureless country. Like all the watering-holes, it catered for every need of the traveller. A shower, a drink, a telephone and, when Mick Murphy had been out on the lake, it provided the rare luxury of fresh fish on the menu. A place not to be missed, because it was the only place there was.

It was dusk when Ray Mead turned the road train off the bitumen and brought it to a halt in a cloud of dust which drew shafts of light from the bar windows. A group of about thirty Aborigines squatted on the sparse grass under a tree opposite the verandah, passing a bottle of port from one to another.

As Mead headed for the bar a frail, grotesque figure in baggy shorts, tattered shirt and a shredded straw hat staggered out from behind the squeaky flyscreen door and stood teetering precariously on the edge of the verandah. Peering out into the growing darkness through what must have been a home-made pair of wire spectacles, he took the cigarette from his mouth to make an announcement, apparently to the world at large.

'A shag has a wonderful life,' he yelled into the night.

There was a stir among the Aborigines while the old man gulped in his breath and swayed back on his feet in preparation for delivering the next line.

'Nothing to do but sit on a rock all day and dive for fish. So cool, so cool.'

Mead stopped in his tracks as a young Aborigine ran past him carrying a bucket of water, followed by a giggling bunch of naked black children.

'Where's my wave?' called the drunk, pushing the cigarette back between his lips and puffing at it rapidly with an exaggerated grin.

The water hit him full in the face to howls of delight from the Aborigines under the tree.

'Thank you,' he said, removing the soggy cigarette. He turned and tottered back into the bar with water dripping from his hat and shorts as Mead followed him, almost stepping on a chicken trying to get out as they walked in.

'S'wonderful,' said the old man, peering up at him in a futile attempt to focus through wet spectacles.

'S'marvellous,' Mead agreed.

There was a lively crowd inside. Mead ripped the pull-top from his can of beer and leaned back on the bar to take in the scene. Two young cattle-station hands were hustling the tourists at the pool table, a couple was swaying slowly on the bare wooden floorboards to the beat of the juke-box, and Merle the Pearl was still propositioning the truckies with a marked lack of success as she wiped over the tables and served up their evening meal. Murphy's mangy-looking dog was asleep at the foot of a fan standing at the end of the bar. There were plenty of familiar faces, and Lightning was on his usual stool at the end of the bar. The staff were under strict instructions to stop serving him when he fell off, which he did most nights at about 11.30 p.m.

'Where you been, Shorty?' he greeted Mead. 'Haven't seen you for ages.'

'I've been stuck at Wauchope for three nights. That's where I've been,' Mead growled.

'No, I don't mean just now. I mean lately. You know. The last few months.'

'Been pushing on, which is what you ought to try doing.'

Lightning ignored the remark and pulled Mead closer to him with a confidential wink.

'Well, you sure missed out, old buddy,' he told him. 'We had a couple of Sydney sheilas here for three bloody weeks. The boys were feeding 'em beans, and Christ did they put on a turn! Once they got going they'd take on every bloke in the bar.'

'Yeah, I heard about them down the road.'

'That was the trouble. Every bastard heard about 'em. Murph had to tell 'em to move on in the end. It was getting too much of a good thing.'

The dancing couple half unwrapped themselves and headed towards the bar, the girl, looking half asleep, still resting her head on her partner's shoulder.

'Well, well, well. Look who's here,' Mead said almost inaudibly.

Lightning looked round.

'Who? The bird with Smithy you mean?'

Mead nodded and grinned.

'Name's Jenny. We got to know each other down the track a bit.'

The brightness had gone from her eyes. She was standing right next to him without seeing him. He reached out and shook her shoulder.

'Hey, who's pushing?' she asked looking at him with such difficulty he might have been swaying from the ceiling.

'It's your old mate Ray. Remember me?'

She stared blankly for a moment and then lay back on Smithy's shoulder.

'Go away. I'm going to bed,' she sighed.

Mead looked at Smithy's hand gently squeezing the girl's breast through her blouse.

'What's she on?' he asked.

'Pot.' Smithy pulled the girl closer to him. 'Makes you real cuddly, doesn't it, darling?' She nodded against his shoulder.

A burly full-blood Aborigine with a grey stubble of beard and his stomach bulging over the waist of his trousers walked up to the bar.

'Give us a bottle of port, Murphy.'

'Have you got any money?' asked the proprietor in his sing-song Irish brogue.

'You know I ain't got no money, but we drunk the last bottle.'

Murphy waved him away.

'If you've got no money you get no port.'

'Chalk it up like you did the last one, you bloody Irish-man.'

'Jesus, what do you think I'm running here? A bloody charity?' Murphy pointed at the board behind the bar. 'Look at it. You owe me your next welfare cheque already.'

'Come on, Murphy. Just one more bottle.'

'No way. I've had enough.'

The Aborigine looked round the bar despairingly, wiping a palm on his grubby yellow shirt.

'Just one more, Murphy. That's all.'

The little old man with the home-made spectacles joined in the argument, trying valiantly not to slur his words.

'Give the poor bugger a drink,' he called. 'He's as sober as I am.'

Murphy gave a sigh of resignation.

'Mother of Mary, what am I doing in a place like this?' He reached behind the bar and grabbed a bottle of port by the neck. 'I'll give you one on condition. You take that mob away back to camp. They've had enough for tonight.'

The Aborigine gently took the bottle from him.

'You're a good man, Murphy,' he smiled as he turned to walk away.

'That's the last one,' Murphy yelled after him. 'So help me, Jesus, that's the last one.'

Mead had his eyes fixed on the blonde behind the bar. Her blouse was unbuttoned low and he could see her nipples at times as she moved.

'I'll have to fight that black bastard next time,' Murphy said to no one in particular. 'When I can't use me fists anymore I'll have to get out of this place. Thank Christ they only send in one bloke at a time. If they had the sense to all come at once they'd kill me. I had 'em knocking on me door at seven o'clock the other morning.'

Mead nudged Lightning.

'Now that is nice,' he breathed, nodding towards the barmaid. 'I like that. I like that very much.'

Merle leaned towards him confidentially as she pushed some dirty plates across from the customer side of the bar.

'Don't waste your time, darling,' she advised, pushing a heavy breast solidly against his elbow. 'She's a mere child. What a big handsome, forceful man like you needs is a real woman. Some experience. Some class.'

She made a show of easing the dress from her great shoulders, staring up at him with a mock expression of seduction, her jaw dropping slack and tongue licking a hairy upper lip.

'Are you getting the message?'

Mead pretended alarm, stepping back sharply and looking towards the door.

'You've got the husky voice real great now, Merle, but you still need that face-lift.'

'Don't try to fight it, baby. You're not fooling anyone,' she told him. 'I finish at eleven,' she added with a grotesque wink.

She sprinted to the door to intercept a truckie who was about to walk out, placing her massive form in front of him with arms outstretched.

'Nobody leaves until Merle gets a man,' she yelled.

He tickled her underneath the arms and slapped her behind as she wriggled away from him.

'Do you really think a face-lift would help?' she asked Mead. 'I mean, once they start lifting where's it all going to end?' She rubbed her bottom thoughtfully.

'Listen, Merle, you can't do that or you'll lose your commission from the haulage companies,' Lightning told her straight-faced.

'She's the only thing that keeps the trucks moving on

this section of the road,' he informed the bar in general.

'Pig! I wish I could keep your lazy behind moving!'

Mead chuckled to himself. Old Lightning was renowned as the slowest man on the road. He would regularly take three or four weeks to complete the run between Darwin and Adelaide which everyone else could do comfortably in five days, even allowing for a few beers along the way. The other drivers were always being asked to look out for him and to prise him out of the particular bar where he had settled. They handed him final ultimatums from the haulage companies, sobered him up and ordered the proprietor to serve him no more booze, which usually succeeded in moving him along the road a way, if only as far as the next bar. On his last trip the finance company had sent up a man to repossess his truck. He climbed into the cab and drove it away while Lightning was in the bar having his usual morning heart-starter with Murphy. That was two months ago, and now he seemed to be a permanent part of the furnishings at Elliott, doing a few odd jobs about the place for his keep and pocket money.

A big truckie thumped his fist down on his table, rattling the cutlery on the laminated surface.

'Merle! Where the hell is my bloody meal?'

She answered like the blast of a ship's fog-horn.

'Shut that noise, you great slob! You're drowning out the juke-box. What do you think this place is anyway, a restaurant?'

She turned to Mead apologetically.

'Darling, can you bear to be without me for a moment?' An exaggerated hint of triumph crept into her voice. 'I'm wanted.'

She touched him softly on the wrist and returned to her huskiest tones. 'Don't worry. I'll be very gentle with you.'

Jenny was giggling.

'He's the one who raped me,' she said, pointing lazily at Mead.

'Stop boasting,' Merle told her. 'What have you got that I couldn't get with a bit more exercise?'

Another truckie was taking an interest in Jenny now. Smithy was on the dance floor with one of the waitresses.

'Come on. Let's go for a little walk,' the truckie suggested. With his arm round Jenny he guided her towards the door, winking back over his shoulder to Mead. 'Tell Smithy I'll bring her back in a minute.'

The barmaid served Mead another can.

'Hope she enjoys it,' she grinned.

Mead looked suggestively at her breasts.

'You've got much more personality,' he told her without lifting his eyes. 'How about the three of us going for a little walk?'

She flashed him a broad smile.

'Down, boy! I just hand out drinks over the bar.'

'Then come out from behind it.'

She looked at him uncertainly.

'I might later on, when Mrs Murphy comes out of the kitchen.

Mead was enjoying himself. He ordered a T-bone steak, medium-rare, with mushrooms. It was the first time for months he had been able to relax on the trip north. He dared not call in at the watering-holes when he had a load of squawking birds on board. Now the beer was getting to him, the party was developing as more trucks rolled in, and the barmaid was definitely giving him a bit of a show. When a bird wears her skirt as short as that and flashes her tits in a bar full of truckies, a man has to be in with a show. He decided to make a night of it.

Murphy switched off the juke-box and got out his piano-accordion, and a young half-caste left the corner card school to demonstrate his party trick of balancing beer cans on his head, which earned him a noisy round of applause.

Murphy's dog stirred irritably in its sleep.

A teenage girl in faded jeans and a dirty T-shirt came up to Mead at the bar. He had noticed her earlier, dancing with her butchy-looking girlfriend. Their knapsacks, with blankets strapped on top, were leaning against the wall by the table where they had eaten their meal.

'Are you going north?' she asked him.

'Sure.'

'Could you give us a lift to Darwin? That's me and my girlfriend over there.'

Mead glanced across and saw the girlfriend watching them. The girl leaned against him and he put his arm round her shoulder.

'Maybe. How old are you, darling?'

'Eighteen.'

'That's okay, but I can't take both of you. You know, three's a crowd and all that.'

She was working a thigh into his crotch.

'We'd give you a good time. Have you got any beans? We really flip out on beans.'

'Sorry, darling, you've picked the wrong man. Anyway, I'm not aiming to leave until morning.'

He lifted her away from him and watched her walking back to her table.

'That's gaol-bait,' he told the barmaid.

'She's a hot little number,' she agreed. 'Perhaps you should have taken up her offer. They could have given you an interesting ride.'

'I like my women one at a time,' he said. 'Gives me a chance to give them my full attention.'

'Listen to the great lover,' she mocked.

Later, when they were dancing, she was soft and

pliant in his arms. She twined both arms about his neck as his mouth brushed her ear. Above them a worn ceiling fan squeaked a persistent protest disturbingly out of time with the rhythm of Murphy's accordion.

'It's not exactly the Ritz,' Mead whispered.

'Does it matter?' She raised her face from his shoulder and her mouth opened as he kissed her. Her body moved instinctively towards him and they stopped pretending to dance.

Someone tapped Mead on the shoulder.

'This is an excuse me, isn't it?'

Mead looked round. 'Piss off, Smithy.'

The girl drew away from him, wiping her mouth with the back of her hand.

'It certainly is.' Smithy took her in his arms. 'The dancing I mean,' she laughed, turning her face away quickly as he sought her lips.

Mead strolled towards the bar where Lightning was trying to get back on to his stool while Mrs Murphy watched him with the kind of expectant attention normally reserved for a juggling act.

Murphy had to break off the music to fuel up a south-bound truck, and the barmaid got away from Smithy. Ignoring Mead, she ducked under the flap at the end of the bar and disappeared into the kitchen. He studied her legs as she went. He decided there was no point in staying sober.

'What's with that sheila anyway? Does she dish it out or doesn't she?'

Lightning grinned at him, lurching forward on his seat.

'I ain't heard no complaints. She's just choosy, that's all. Maybe you ain't wearing the right after-shave.'

Jenny was prancing about the floor, on another high, head back, arms outstretched, floating on the music in her mind while the truckies clapped encouragement.

It was close to one o'clock when Mead went to the outside lavatory. Large moths were fluttering against the bare light bulb, throwing trembling shadows on the dust. The night was hot and still, pulsating with the sound of cicadas. He heard the clatter of a garbage-can lid in the backyard and saw a slim figure move across the light of the kitchen window.

'Are you coming back to finish our dance?' he called softly. She stood waiting for him and he took her in his arms.

'I've got to finish cleaning up.'

He pushed her gently back against the wall, out of the light. Her body was responding again. He undid the bottom buttons of her blouse and slipped his hand inside. She was kissing him greedily now as he pressed himself urgently into her. She gasped as he broke away from her and peeled open her blouse.

'You want it. Let's go to your room.'

'No. We can't. I share with the other girl.'

'So what?' Mead growled.

'Look, could you give me a ride? I've got a few days off owing to me. I want to go up to Darwin.'

He hesitated.

'I want to, honestly.' She pulled his face to hers and bit his lip gently. 'We can't here. The Murphys.'

'When can you get away?'

'Give me about a quarter of an hour. Go back inside and have another beer. Then I'll be ready.'

She hurried away leaving Mead in the dark.

In Murphy's office she picked up the phone and spun the handle to raise the operator. There was a long pause before a sleepy voice asked her for the number. She waited impatiently on the silent line.

'Go ahead, caller,' said the operator.

'Hello, Mike?' she said urgently, keeping her voice low.

He sounded half asleep. She must have woken him up.

'It's Julie.' She paused 'Mike, I've got him. His name's Mead. Ray Mead. The truck's here now. Registration SRH 753. You got that?'

She glanced over her shoulder at the door.

'Sure I'm sure. He's got a specially-built compartment right behind the driver's cab. I took a look through the top and its full of empty cages.'

In the bar, Mrs Murphy came round from behind the counter.

'Give me a hand to put him away for the night,' she said, bending to lift Lightning from the floor.

Mead grabbed the other arm and between them they hauled the sagging man to his room.

'I'll take a bottle of brandy with me, Mrs Murphy, just to keep me company on the road,' he told her.

She laughed at him.

'You're not fooling me, Ray Mead,' she chided, wagging a podgy finger at him. 'I know you'll be taking Julie with you. Mind you, I don't know what the gal sees in you. For m'self I wouldn't touch you with a tow-bar!'

Chapter Nine

Ex-policewoman Julie Henderson looked at it this way—if you had to screw to do your job you might as well make the most of it.

One of the side benefits of a strict Catholic upbringing was that it heightened the enjoyment of sin. When it came to whetting the appetite for indulgence, nothing could match a cloistered adolescence. Those whispered anticipations in the darkness of the dormitories were obscene enough to ease youthful impatience as growth slowly lowered the convent walls, but they presented maturity with the problem of reconciling imagination with the reality of the outside world.

Her mother was not happy when her blossoming, vulnerable daughter decided to apply for a cadetship at the police academy. As she pointed out to the girl, it would bring her into contact with vulgarities and unpleasantness beyond her imagination which would cause her quite unnecessary distress. That convinced Julie she was on the right track. She could walk through degradation with right on her side. After all, wasn't that what she had been taught to expect of life?

When Alan Coates was recruiting in 1970 for his newly formed Federal Narcotics Bureau, she jumped at the chance to get out of uniform and into undercover work. It was not just that promotion chances for a woman were limited in the New South Wales police force or that there was a tendency to use her more as a social worker than a law enforcement officer. What appealed to her was the duality of the job. She could act the whore, she could lie, she could even indulge in a little communal pot-smoking, getting her kicks vicariously while still retaining her official parachute of respectability. It gave her a moral licence to live out her convent fantasies. She was very good at her work.

So here she was, playing out her role as the truckie's pick-up, roaring through the outback night with a complete stranger at the wheel, her bare feet pressed against the dashboard as she leaned back in the passenger seat so that a long expanse of leg was gently illuminated by the lights of the control panel.

Mead glanced across at her as the cab was lit up by the headlights of an approaching road train. Her legs were parted slightly as she sipped at a can of beer. She looked completely relaxed. He grinned to himself as the orange trailer lights of the other road train flashed past. She was a worthy consolation prize for the five thousand dollars he was going to miss out on this trip.

'We'll get down the road a bit and then pull over for a few hours,' he told her.

'Do you need some sleep, you poor thing?' she asked with mock concern.

He laughed. 'I like a girl with a sense of humour!'

She admired the skill with which he handled the big truck, pushing it fast along the endless bitumen, sweeping through the bends, alert all the time for animals on the road. There was no sign of tiredness or the effects of the beer he had drunk. His cigarette glowed in the dark as the wheels consumed the miles.

She left him to his concentration and absorbed herself in the charm of the night. They were still far enough south to enjoy the cool darkness of the desert pouring in through open windows. She could see the outlines of sparsely timbered hills around them against the backdrop of a starlit sky.

Gradually a soft, ruddy glow materialised in the distance ahead, lighting a long length of the horizon.

'Bushfire,' said Mead. 'Looks as though we're going to run right into it.'

There was no other traffic on the road, only rabbits and mice scurrying away as though they were scorched by the headlights and occasionally a snake lashing itself clear, transparent and fast as a splash of water.

Julie felt the drag of the engine brake as Mead lifted his foot from the accelerator. At first she thought he had decided to pull in for the night, but then she saw about a dozen kangaroos sit up in the scrub alongside the road.

'They're a fucking menace,' Mead complained. 'If you hit one of those big reds you can say goodbye to your radiator for sure.'

The mob broke up suddenly and several of the kangaroos bounded across the road in front of the truck. Mead cursed, braking violently as he blasted the horn.

'They're gorgeous,' Julie told him. 'Look at that lovely little joey. He's completely lost.'

'It's the bitumen that attracts them. The run-off of the rain creates a strip of nice green feed on either side that brings them in for miles. That's why you see so many dead ones along the highway. I've even seen them licking up the rain off the road.'

A road works diversion took them along a rough track for a couple of miles, jolting Julie's feet from the dashboard and making her hang on to her seat as the truck shuddered over the corrugations.

They could see the flames now blood red in the distance.

'I reckon that would be a thirty-mile front and moving pretty fast,' Mead told her.

'How do they start?'

'Lightning, maybe. The sun on a piece of glass, or maybe some idiot chucking a cigarette end out of the window, or just a piece of hot carbon fired out from a diesel exhaust. There are fires burning all the time up here. They keep going until the rain stops them or they run into the desert.'

'Wouldn't anyone be trying to put it out?'

'There's not much they can do more than protecting the homesteads. They're the main worry. That fire's probably moving faster than a man can run.'

'The poor animals,' Julie murmured.

'Watch out and you might see some of them trying to outrun it. Sometimes you see a rabbit all on fire like a flaming torch, I've seen them carry the fire from one side of the track to the other like that.'

The sweet smell of burning bush was strong in the air as they neared the front of the fire. It was thinner on the ground than it had looked from a distance advancing not in a wall of flame, as Julie had imagined, but in a seeping fashion like a tide coming over mud flats with isolated pools of flame well ahead of the main flow.

Fascinated, she watched them rapidly linking up as yellow flames raced across the thin white grass. In the darkness awaiting the fire, gum trees suddenly exploded in balls of flame as though a match had been set to a primed torch. To the horizon trees stood out as flaring pillars of flame like yellow beacons on a red sea.

The road ahead was a black pathway through the fire. It surrounded them completely, reaching to the horizon in every direction. Julie could see Mead grinning to himself in the glow of the flames.

'Don't worry, love. It's a way of life out here,' he told her, obviously amused at her reaction to the size of the fire. 'Those trees need a bushfire to re-seed themselves. Only fire can release the seeds.'

Incredibly, it seemed to Julie, some trees escaped untouched, the flames had moved on so quickly. They reached briefly up to snatch the flimsy creepers from the trunk, then dropped back to the undergrowth without igniting the upper branches, although all around them stood blackened, smoking skeletons.

As the front of the fire was left far behind them, Julie stared in fascination at a hypnotic display of deep red embers glowing in the blackness as if she was flying across the sprinkled lights of some great city.

'It's beautiful,' she murmured.

'We'll call it a night when we get into unburnt country,' Mead remarked.

He pulled the truck off the highway at the first opportunity and as soon as the engine died Julie climbed down from the cabin to stretch herself in the sudden stillness of the night.

She liked his hands on her body. She responded hungrily to his kiss. He treated her, touched her, as though she were his property and there were no questions to be asked.

'Get in the cot.' He indicated the bunk at the rear of the cabin. 'I'm just going to check the load.'

Her blouse was already undone. She took it off and slipped out of her skirt as she watched the light of his torch moving along the trailers.

The sense of total isolation, now that the noise and the movement had stopped, was too strong to be ignored. The distant silence of the bush night reached out to brush her nakedness with the cool fiingers of a gentle breeze.

She wanted to experience the strength of him, to taste the salt on his skin and to feel the roughness of his face against her cheeks. For a while he would know the truth of her.

She was lying on the bunk when he climbed back into the cabin. He studied her in the softness of the light and as she watched him she felt her body flexing under his gaze.

He smiled at her and stripped off his clothes.

'You are delicious,' he told her with obvious sincerity.

She opened her arms to him.

'Then come and taste me.'

He was quick the first time but she soon roused him again to satisfy her own desire, breathing her lust into his ear to urge him on and matching the violence of his passion with her own.

The nail of her forefinger traced a circle on his shoulder as he lay beside her in the darkness. She could not tell if he was asleep.

'Ray.'

He stirred slightly and answered her wearily, with a hint of irritation.

'What do you want?'

'When we get to Darwin could you put me in touch with someone in the drug scene? You know, a pusher. I want to get hold of some stuff to take back with me.'

'Don't know anybody.'

'Oh, come on, you must do. You've got plenty of contacts in Darwin. You must know someone who can put me in touch with someone. Do me a favour, will you?'

'I told you, darling. I don't know anybody. It's not my scene, okay?'

He rolled over to turn his back on her.

'Now go to sleep. We've got an early start in the morning.'

Mead's alarm clock woke them before first light and he drove a hundred miles through lightly timbered bush before stopping to cook breakfast at the roadside.

By 11 a.m. they were crossing the old steel-framed railway bridge across the narrow Katherine River.

'This is a hit or miss job,' Mead told her as he swung the rumbling road train on to the approach ramp. 'Do you want to get out and walk across?'

She shook her head, but his eyes were glued on the impossibly narrow entrance to the bridge as he concentrated on placing his wheels precisely astride the single railway track.

'Yes or no?' he snapped.

'No.'

He chuckled.

'Your lifebelt's under your seat.'

He was enjoying demonstrating his expertise. Without hesitation he eased the road train on to the bridge. There were about three inches to spare on either side as it rolled across the rattling planks.

From the height of her side window, Julie could not see the bridge at all. She looked straight to the torpid, brown water far below her flowing out of the Katherine Gorge.

There was a car stationary in the middle of the road on the far side of the bridge. It was surrounded by a jostling group of about forty Aborigines who were pressing in on an elderly tourist couple and trying to sell them hand-painted boomerangs and spears. The woman was still sitting in the car but her husband had got out and was arguing with the blacks, who had encircled him so that only his pale face and grey hair was visible through the boomerangs being pushed towards him. He was looking very harassed as the truck approached but he managed to get an arm free to wave towards it.

Mead was still working his way up through the gears. He punched out two explosive blasts on the main horn which scattered the rear ranks of the Aborigines from his path and waved back at the old man.

'Collecting toll today, I see,' he remarked, grinning across at Julie.

'Don't you think we should stop and give the old couple a hand?'

The suggestion seemed to surprise him.

'What for? No, bugger 'em. They're tourists. They came on this road looking for adventure and something to tell their mates back home about and now they've found it. Anyway, it's only a road tax like I have to pay, only this time the Government ain't the robbers.'

'Why on earth did they stop?' Julie asked, still thinking about the expression on the old man's face when he realised the truck was not going to pull up.

'When they link arms and stretch themselves across the road you haven't got much choice unless you're going to run right over 'em.'

'You're a callous bastard,' she told him, with feeling.

He reached across and patted her thigh.

'That's right, darling. And you're better at using your fanny than your head, so why don't you just stick to screwing?'

It was late afternoon as they wound their way through the wild wooded hills south of Darwin. The humidity had risen sharply and Julie's blouse was wet with perspiration despite the air conditioning in the cab.

'Will I see you in town tonight?' she asked.

'I doubt it, darling. I've got to get these trailers unloaded as soon as we get there, and then I'll be going round to the girlfriend's place.'

'Will she be working tonight?'

Mead nodded. 'I guess so.'

'Do you reckon you could find me somewhere to stay?'

'Oh, sure! I'll just say to Karen, "This is the bird I screwed on the road last night and do you mind if she sleeps with us tonight?" No way, honey. I don't even want to know you.'

Julie pretended to ponder the situation for a while.

'Do you think I might pick up something at the

116

Capricorn? There would be a few single blokes around there, wouldn't there?'

'Sure. I don't think you'd have any worries.'

'I might see you there tonight, then.'

'Please yourself, if you've got nowhere better to go.'

Rain was streaming from the sky in a noisy torrent as they passed the naval communications centre on the outskirts of Darwin and started to move through scattered, outer suburban development. Despite the wipers, Julie could see little through the flow of water on the windscreen beyond the tail lights of the car in front as it groped its way cautiously through the greyness of the rain and the flooded roadway.

Mead dropped her at Winnellie, opposite the airport.

'I turn off the highway here,' he told her. 'The city centre's only a couple of miles down the road and you should have no trouble getting a lift this time of day. The factories are knocking off, and there'll be plenty of cars going that way.'

She took her case from him and was taken by surprise by the blast of hot air as she opened the cab door. There was nowhere to shelter from the rain. She stood on the footpath watching the length of trailers move slowly past until they disappeared in a mist of spray. The grey shape of a car came slowly out of the rain behind it and she stepped forward on to the road waving eagerly for it to stop. To her relief, it did. She snatched the door open and almost fell inside.

'Miss Henderson, you look a mess!'

She looked up into Mike Lindsay's smiling face.

'Mike!' She brushed the water from her arms. 'Lucky you happened to be passing!'

'All part of the service,' he grinned.

'I picked you up at Berrimah. Do you know which depot he's going to?'

She shook her head.

'No, he didn't say.'

'Okay. We'll just see where he's dropping his load and then I'll get you to a nice dry motel room.'

Ahead of them Mead's truck turned off the main road and Lindsay followed it through the drab back streets of an industrial area.

'I'm afraid I didn't find out very much, Mike,' Julie told him apologetically. 'His name is Ray Mead, he runs his own haulage business with the one truck, lives in Adelaide, married with a couple of young kids, and he's very keen on a girlfriend in Darwin who's a dancer at a local nightclub.'

'Capricorn Club?'

'Yeah, how d'you know that?'

'It's the only one here.'

'Oh,' said Julie with a smile. 'Her name's Karen.'

'I know.'

She looked at him curiously.

'It seems I haven't found out much you didn't know already.'

'Yes you have. It's just that it's all starting to come together. You were the one who found Mead, and that was the job you set out to do. I'd hate you to think you had wasted your time, especially after the price you paid.'

'What do you mean?'

She knew what he was getting at as soon as she said it but too late. She had fallen for it.

'Well you've obviously suffered a very nasty bite on the neck,' said Lindsay, straight-faced.

She blushed and raised a hand to the spot.

'Dental check,' she told him. 'Thought it might help with identification.'

He laughed.

'Clever, Miss Henderson, but a trifle over-enthusiastic in view of the fact that his phone number's written on the side of his truck.'

He pointed to the truck ahead as it turned right into a freight yard.

'Transcontinental Freight. Well, no doubt they will be able to keep us pretty well informed of Mead's time schedules from now on.'

He drove past the yard without changing speed then turned back towards the main highway.

'Okay, now we can get you to that motel,' he told her with a smile. 'Do you know how long he is staying in town?'

'Not long. He's hoping to be leaving for Adelaide tomorrow morning. It depends on how quickly he can get unloaded. He said he's only got a few cars to load for the return run.'

'Yes, he won't waste much time. He's running a couple of days behind schedule and he won't want to miss the next consignment. He would have lost out on a lot of money this trip.'

Lindsay was deep in thought as they drove towards the city. It was Julie who broke the silence.

'Do you want me to take a look at the Capricorn Club tonight?'

'No. We'll keep out of their way now. We've got everything we need at this end. Tomorrow you go back to Canberra and, in the meantime, we sit down and work out a nice full report for you to take back with you for Alan Coates.'

'What about you, Mike? Aren't you going back too?'

Lindsay shook his head.

'I've got a few things to tie up here and then I go down to Adelaide. I want to take a look at Mr Mead's home base and find out how the syndicate gives him his instructions.'

'Do you think he's the only truckie they're using?'

Lindsay turned the car into the forecourt of the Buffalo Motel.

'I'm sure of it,' he replied. 'And next trip we take him.'

Chapter Ten

Soon after midday on 19 December the teleprinter in Federal Narcotics Bureau Canberra headquarters burst into life. It rapped out the incoming message at a hundred words a minute. The girl whose job it was to tear off the messages and deliver them to the appropriate offices let it run for a few seconds before getting up from her typewriter and strolling across to the machine. She read casually through Mike Lindsay's report as the paper jerked upwards to accommodate the final lines and the teleprinter suddenly lapsed back into silence.

FEDERAL NARCOTICS BUREAU, CANBERRA
URGENT ATTENTION DIRECTOR
EX LINDSAY COM POLICE OFFICE, ADELAIDE

MEAD LOADED FREIGHT AND LEFT
ADELAIDE NORTHBOUND AT 1000 HOURS
TODAY. RV WITH TRAPPERS SET FOR
23 DECEMBER AT POWELL CREEK, NT.
AIRCRAFT DUE 1200 HOURS 25 DECEMBER.
BURROWS STAYING BUFFALO MOTEL,
DARWIN.

PROPOSE TO APPREHEND MEAD AND
ACCOMPLICES AT POWELL CREEK THEN
PROCEED WITH TRUCK TO AIRSTRIP FOR RV
WITH AIRCRAFT AND APPREHENSION OF
PILOT AND BURROWS.

REQUIRE:

1.   ASSISTANCE OF FAUNA OFFICER AND
     EXPERIENCED DRIVER FOR KENWORTH
     K125 TRUCK AT POWELL CREEK. FAUNA
     OFFICER TO TAKE CUSTODY OF BIRDS.

2.   POLICE VEHICLE AND DRIVER FROM
     ALICE SPRINGS TO ASSIST IN ESCORT OF
     PRISONERS TO DARWIN.

3   ASSISTANCE FRANK ADAMS AND
     ANOTHER OFFICER EX DARWIN AT
     AIRSTRIP.

PROPOSE 1 AND 2 RV ALICE SPRINGS
     21 DECEMBER.

AWAIT THIS OFFICE FOR YOUR
CONFIRMATION.

MESSAGE ENDS

Senior Inspector Peter Jamieson was in Alan Coates's office within an hour of the telex being placed on the bureau director's desk. He fumbled for his spectacles in the breast pocket of his safari uniform while he peered at the vague outlines of the words on the paper Coates had pushed across the desk towards him. It really could not have come at a more inopportune time. He was busy preparing the National Fauna Squad's first report to C.O.N.C.O.M.—the Council of Nature Conservation Ministers. It was quite vital.

'Our man in Darwin is involved in a court hearing at the moment,' he told Coates wearily. 'It may continue next week so I can't possibly have him coming down to Alice on Saturday.'

'What about the Territory wildlife people? Couldn't they send out a vehicle from Alice?'

'Well, I suppose so, but I really feel the N.E.S. should be involved in this.'

Coates waited while Jamieson frowned at the telex, fidgeting in his chair with irritating indecision.

'I agree with you, Inspector, but how you handle it is entirely up to you,' Coates said. 'I'm wiring approval of Lindsay's proposals. What I need to know is who you are going to send along.'

'I'll check with Alice and see how they're situated. It would mean tying up a man and vehicle for several days as he would have to drive the birds up to Darwin for court evidence. I don't know if they'd have anyone available to do that.'

'Would you confirm the arrangement with me as soon as possible?' Coates asked. 'This is a major operation for us and I want to give Lindsay all the back-up he requires.'

Jamieson nodded, still appearing uncertain. Coates smiled sympathetically.

'It's a pity you've got to hand it over to the local boys. It would be a real feather in your cap to come up with a catch like this in your first two months of operation.'

'Perhaps I should go myself,' Jamieson suggested.

Coates raised his eyebrows and studied him solemnly.

'I think that would be a very good idea, Inspector,' he said.

Mike Lindsay was far from happy at the thought of working in the field with Jamieson. All he had wanted was a junior officer to take the birds off his hands once he had arrested Mead. That way he would have remained clearly in charge of the operation. Now here was Jamieson, stepping briskly across the Alice Springs tarmac in his crisp new uniform with its colourful boy scout shoulder-flash, looking as though he was arriving for an investiture.

Nothing had been said about their respective ranks. As a Bureau man, Lindsay was rated simply as an investigator. He had left his Detective-Superintendent title behind with the New South Wales Police. He suspected that they shared the same Public Service grade but Jamieson had the advantage of a uniform, a rank and the right to claim that this section of the operation was more in his line than in Lindsay's. He had all the symptoms of a severe attack of empire building. Lindsay wished to hell Coates had made it clear who was boss. He decided on the friendly approach.

'Welcome to the Red Heart,' he smiled as Jamieson entered the terminal building. 'Did you have a good flight?'

Jamieson shook his hand and nodded. 'Thank you, yes. I only had a half-hour wait in Sydney. It's very good of you to meet me, Mr Lindsay.'

'Mike,' said Lindsay.

Alice Springs had lost its quaintness as the isolated centre of the Australian wilderness. It was no longer a one-horse town, a dusty main street flanked by sagging verandahs. International tourism had brought a peculiar sophistication to the place, still small by city standards but beyond the days of being just a cattlemen's town. Now the Aborigines sold their boomerangs and nulla-nullas from a glass-fronted craft centre close by the smart shopping arcades, and a Dutch artist in a palatial gallery auctioned instant paintings to coach-loads of tourists who instructed him as he painted, detailing the scene they wanted right down to the position of the final tree.

'You can see this place growing every time you come

back to it,' Jamieson remarked as they drove through the gap in the range of bare craggy hills which hid the town from the airport.

'It's certainly gone ahead since the Americans opened up the Pine Gap tracking station,' Lindsay agreed.

Jamieson assumed a more formal tone.

'Are all the arrangements in hand? The director did not have much time to set them up.'

Lindsay glanced away from the road momentarily to look at him.

'A driver for the truck is coming down from Darwin on this afternoon's flight. Everything else is organised.'

'How can you be sure the rendezvous dates are right?'

The big ex-cop started gnawing his lower lip. The nerve of the man! Even Coates didn't ask him how he got his information. No doubt he had a good idea, but it was the last thing he wanted to know. Lindsay wondered what Jamieson's reaction would be if he told him about a neat little break-and-entry job, coinciding with Sue Mead's regular morning outing to take her elder boy to school, and the microphone tucked unobstrusively into the mouthpiece of her telephone.

'I'm sure,' he replied.

There was the possibility, of course, that Mead was instructed to add a specified number of days to the dates that Burrows had telephoned him from Sydney, but he doubted it. Mead's trailers were loaded and ready to go when the call came through, and he left immediately. If he did not have to reach Powell Creek until after the twenty-third there was no need to hurry.

'Would they need two people to trap the birds or would one man be able to handle it on his own?' he asked Jamieson.

'Normally you could expect to find a pair of trappers. There's a fair bit of work involved. The nets are not easy to handle. They have to be repaired regularly, the birds have to be watered and fed, and with two drivers they can drive virtually non-stop back to the city.'

'But in this case Mead does the driving.'

'And he must water and feed on the road.'

'Right. A trapper would have plenty of time between pick-ups to get himself organised. He's got a fortnight to stock up on supplies, pick the best spot to spread his nets and gather his catch.'

Lindsay turned the Range Rover off the highway on to a road which ran alongside the dry, dusty bed of the Todd River.

'He'd have time to pick and choose, to select the very best birds,' Jamieson added.

'Yes. This is a very smooth operation. My feeling is that there is only one trapper out there, but we will have to be prepared for more.'

Lindsay stopped the vehicle to let a line of chattering Aboriginal children cross the road hand-in-hand as their teacher urged them to hurry.

'I'd like to be on the road for Powell Creek by 5 a.m. tomorrow,' he told Jamieson. 'We must pick up the trapper before dark as Mead could arrive before first light on Monday.'

'You intend to take the prisoners by road from Powell Creek to Darwin?'

Lindsay nodded.

'We should be able to do it comfortably in ten hours and have Mead and his mate safely locked up in Fannie Bay gaol for Christmas. That will give me at least twenty-four hours in Darwin to organise a reception committee for the plane when it comes in on the twenty-fifth.'

A thousand miles to the north, as Lindsay and Jamieson were turning into the drive of their Alice Springs motel, John Clements, the senior duty meteorologist at

Darwin's Tropical Cyclone Warning Centre, was studying weather satellite photographs of a tropical disturbance developing over the Arafura Sea.

It was a routine watch, one of the chores of the cyclone season.

The infra-red pictures from the United States satellite N.O.A.A. 4 had been received during the morning monitoring a tropical low between Timor and West Irian, the area in which Cyclone Selma had formed less than three weeks earlier. The low had developed four hundred and forty miles north-east of Darwin and was now moving slowly south-westwards.

Clements was half an hour late back from lunch. He studied the latest photograph to come in, then put it on top of the others and took them all to the Regional Director.

'It looks as though Selma has got herself a baby sister,' he grinned as he spread them on the director's desk.

At 4 p.m. the Centre alerted outlying communities along the coast to the north-east that there was the possibility of a tropical cyclone developing. Ships in the Arafura and Timor Seas began transmitting three-hourly weather and radar rain reports to Weather Darwin.

Within six hours it was clear that a cyclone had formed. It was named Tracy.

A cloud of fine white dust floated high in the air behind the road train as Ray Mead swung it off the Stuart Highway bitumen at Powell Creek and on to the dirt track leading to the hidden shores of the lake.

He was feeling more relaxed and happy than he had for a long time. Karen was waiting for him in Darwin. They would spend Christmas night together laughing and making love, knowing that this time he would not have to leave again for Adelaide the next morning.

On the road he had amused himself by imagining her reaction when she saw the opal ring. He had bought the best stone he could find in Coober Pedy and taken it to Adelaide to be polished and set. She would recognise its value. It would be a symbol of their future together.

As he concentrated his thoughts on that moment, as he played a pleasing game in his mind deciding the exact words with which she would greet the gift, anger and pain faded away behind him like the hazy road in his driving mirror.

Now Sue knew. Driving north to Darwin for Christmas, leaving her and the children alone, was the final straw. They were finished. They had nothing left to give each other now but bitterness.

He wished that he never had to return to that house in Adelaide. The truck, more than the house, had been his home in the last few years. There would be no feelings of regret at leaving, not even at turning away from the boys for he had seen little enough of them. But for their mother's assurances, they would probably be unaware that he was their father. In his mind now they were simply her appendages. Once they held his future. Now they clung to his past.

Sue's viciousness had erased his guilt and justified a decision forged by desire and hardened by time. So it was to be after all! His last doubts were gone.

But he could not make the move yet. When he collected his five thousand dollars for this shipment, he would be out of the red, with enough in the bank to pay off the truck. He needed at least another six months to raise finance for two more vehicles and to get the business operating successfully enough to provide him with an income while he and Karen were in Europe.

The road train broke clear of the clinging scrub and

Mead could see Habib's dusty ice-cream van waiting on the banks of the great lake. The cages were already spread across the ground behind the van. Damn the old fool! Mead had told him time and again not to unload them before he arrived just in case someone else happened to breeze along. The old man was sitting at the water's edge, leaning back against a pink-limbed gum tree, a fishing rod in his hand, his grubby hat tilted forward over his forehead. Fish for lunch, thought Mead.

The airbrakes hissed as Mead brought the truck to a halt alongside the van. He swung himself easily from the cab and dropped to the ground. Habib came walking slowly towards him, waving a hand across his face to ward off the bushflies.

'Howya going, you silly old bastard?' Mead called good-naturedly.

He had just got beyond the van when he saw the look in the old man's big brown eyes.

'Sorry, Ray,' he muttered. 'We been rumbled.'

Lindsay stepped from behind the van and had Mead's arms pinned behind his back before he had time to turn round, Mead felt the touch of steel on his wrists and heard the snap of handcuffs.

A four-wheel-drive police vehicle came out of the scrub and pulled up alongside the truck. The back door of the ice-cream van swung open and a lean man in a khaki uniform stepped out. Lindsay pushed Mead towards him.

'Senior Inspector Jamieson, National Fauna Squad,' he told Mead. 'You are under arrest for breaches of the Northern Territory Wildlife Conservation and Control Ordinance and will be taken into custody to Darwin where you will be charged and placed before the court.'

'What are you talking about?' Mead blurted out, taken completely by surprise. Jamieson ignored him.

'You are advised that you are not obliged to say anything at this stage, and anything you do say may be used in evidence at the court hearing,' he continued.

Mead glanced towards the road train. The passenger from the police vehicle had climbed into the cab. He was kneeling on the driver's seat and rummaging through the lockers above the bunk. He looked more like a truckie than a cop.

The shock was hitting Mead. His stomach had screwed up into a tight knot and he felt faint. It all seemed so unreal. A few minutes earlier everything had been so fine. Now his vision of the future had been changed as abruptly as a projector slide on a screen.

'This has got nothing to do with me. I just drive a truck,' he told Jamieson.

'Have you met this man before?' the inspector asked, indicating Habib.

'Sure. I see him now and then. I drop off a few supplies for him.'

'Don't waste our time, Mead,' Lindsay snapped. 'Let's take a look at where you keep the birds.'

Mead stumbled as he was thrust towards the trailers, his hands behind his back. The door on the passenger side of the cab was pushed open and the searching cop called Lindsay.

'There are four of these.' He handed down a grey attaché-case he had taken from the locker over the bunk.

Lindsay stared hard at Mead. 'Business papers?' he asked sarcastically.

He put his foot on to the front wheel hub and placed the case on his knee to open it.

'Mostly empty,' he remarked. He raised it to his face and sniffed inside. 'We'll take all four of them for lab tests,' he told the cop. 'Have you found any keys in there?'

'Yes,' the cop replied, disappearing back into the cab

momentarily. He threw Lindsay a bunch of keys. Lindsay fingered through them and found one to fit the padlock on the bird compartment. He slid open the steel door and looked inside at the rows of empty cages sitting on the fiddled shelves. He stared down at Mead, with Jamieson standing close beside him, and shook his head slowly.

'You're gone, Mead. You're going to be eating your Christmas dinner as a guest of Her Majesty at Fannie Bay.'

He re-locked the compartment door and beckoned Mead to follow him to the rear trailer. Watching for the truckie's reaction he tapped a knuckle on two forty-four-gallon drums.

'And aviation fuel too! You and I are going to have a long chat about all this on the way up to Darwin. You can tell us what personal things you need to take with you and we'll collect them from the truck.'

He turned to Habib who was sitting on the ground beside his van.

'The same goes for you. And you might as well pack up your fishing rod. We've got our catch for today.'

The old man hoisted himself wearily to his feet and walked slowly towards the bank of the lake shaking his head and muttering to himself.

'Only bloody birds. Only bloody birds. Millions of 'm 'ere.'

Darwin's radio programmes were first interrupted by the howl of cyclone warning sirens shortly after midday on Christmas Eve. The pubs were packed with noisy, jostling crowds, the office parties in full swing.

It was a pre-recorded tape, the same one that was played every half-hour over radio and television three weeks earlier when Cyclone Selma was heading towards the city.

131

'A cyclone is imminent. A few hours of organised family action can turn the odds your way. Batten down your house by making sure all doors and windows are securely fastened or strengthened by diagonal strips of heavy adhesive tape. Remove all pictures from walls and all table ornaments. These could be lethal.'

John Clements had never regretted his decision to record the tape himself. The local radio station manager wanted to use the voice of one of his D.J.s but Clements insisted on reading his own script. It turned out he was right. The whole point of the exercise was for the warning to sound different, to attract attention. So instead of the familiar voice of the D.J. breezing through his lines as though he was doing a commercial for a discount store, Clements cut across the programme sounding a trifle unprofessional admittedly, but indisputably urgent.

'When the cyclone comes remain calm and stay inside. Keep a window open on the side away from the wind and remember if the wind drops suddenly the calm eye of the cyclone is probably overhead. As the winds will soon resume abruptly with equal violence from another direction, you must shut that window and open another on the far side of the house. Only go under elevated houses as a last resort. If the building shows signs of breaking up, stand in doorways or shelter in the bathroom.'

They had used the rapid repeat siren of one of the Navy patrol boats to herald the announcement. It sounded like all hell let loose.

No effort was needed for Clements to muster up sincerity. He had been working at the Weather Bureau in Townsville three years earlier when the town had been lashed by the tail of a cyclone which passed by fifty miles away. That had been close enough.

Now, as he looked at the radar screen, he could feel

the skin tighten on the nape of his neck. At dawn Tracy had changed direction from the south-westerly course that would have taken it safely past Darwin. It rounded Bathurst Island and swung straight towards them like a ship coming into harbour.

After analysing the noon chart he had drawn up a Flash Cyclone Warning, a top priority communiqué to the Defence Forces, emergency services, local administrators and the media.

'At twelve noon Central Standard Time severe tropical cyclone Tracy was centred sixty-eight miles west-north-west of Darwin and is now moving slowly south-east closer to Darwin. Very destructive winds of 75 m.p.h. with gusts of 93 m.p.h. have been reported near the centre and are expected in the Darwin area tonight and tomorrow.'

The office junior came back with the beef and tomato sandwiches Clements had ordered for lunch.

'What's going on out there?' Clements asked.

'The rain's settled in and there's a fairly strong wind blowing,' the lad replied.

'The pub's crammed full. They're all singing their heads off.'

'Bloody fools! The director's been trying to raise members of the emergency committee but it seems the whole public service has packed it in for the season. I just rang the Northern Territory Department offices and all I got was some idiot who kept yelling "Happy Christmas". Probably had the typist on his lap and a can of beer in his spare hand.'

Clements walked back to the radar screen.

'Jesus Christ, look at the damn thing! Do they think we're just fooling around?'

The calm central eye of Tracy stared out at him from the top left-hand side of the glowing screen. The cloudy radar echoes from the rain shield wound around the eye in spiral bands that left a tail trailing like a swirling catherine-wheel.

'It's speeded up and intensified since it turned towards us this morning.'

Clements beckoned the lad across to the screen.

'You see the diameter of the eye has decreased to about seven miles. That's a sure sign a cyclone's deepening. The whole echo area is only about ninety-five miles across, which makes her a tight, vicious bitch.'

The telephone on Clements's desk rang and was picked up by a bearded young man who was just walking past with the latest automatic weather station reports in his hand.

'It's for you, John,' he called. 'Frank Adams.'

Clements took the phone from him.

'Frank, old mate! Listen, do you know where the Commissioner is hiding? The director's trying to contact him.'

He reached behind him for his chair.

'Yeah, and a happy Christmas to you too.'

Clements lifted some papers from his desk to search for his pen as Adams was talking.

'Tomorrow! No way! Christ, man, didn't you hear the warning? Believe me, we may not be here tomorrow. You can tell your Canberra mate—he's there with you, is he?—yes, well you can tell him he's picked the wrong Christmas to be in Darwin. We're in for a hell of a night!'

He hung up and turned to the others with a sigh of exasperation.

'Would you believe what he wanted? He wanted to know if there was any possibility of a light aircraft flying in from Kupang tomorrow morning!'

·

Chapter Eleven

In the first minutes of Christmas morning Darwin began to feel the growing fury of Tracy as it bore down on the city with great rolls of thunder and lightning continually illuminating the north-western sky.

Between 9 p.m. and midnight, the wind-driven rain which had been falling all day steadily increased in intensity as the cyclone came closer, and when the outer edge of Tracy's whirling clockwise winds reached the coast it turned to horizontal rain, pounding walls and windows like the jet of a fireman's hose.

There were still crowds drinking in the pubs, the clubs and the wine bars, singing carols with voices lusty enough to drown momentarily the roar of the wind and the thunder, toasting the arrival of Christmas Day, and passing round addresses of parties to go to when the bars closed.

At the Buffalo Motel's Terrace Bar a drunk wearing only a pair of shorts tottered outside waving a can of beer and singing 'Silent Night' to be blown straight into the swimming pool. The room was sprayed with water when he came back through the door and stood dripping in front of his cheering friends.

'Shtill raining out there,' he declared decisively, swaying slightly as he tried to get the crowd into focus.

More than three hundred people had turned up for Midnight Mass at the cathedral, where the situation was growing more chaotic by the minute. Water was running in steady streams down the inside of the walls beneath the high louvre windows and the Bishop had to wade through an ankle-deep pool to reach the high altar.

He considered removing his shoes but decided it would be improper and continued the service with as much dignity as he could muster while walking on his heels.

The restlessness among the congregation increased when louvres began to break and shower on to the stone floor, and then a piece of roofing iron was blown along a side aisle. An elderly woman stood up suddenly and screamed something in Italian before her husband reached up to take her arm and pull her back down to her knees.

When the lights went out, plunging them all into eerie, frightening darkness, the Bishop posted the altar boys by the candles with boxes of matches to relight them as they blew out. Without electricity there was no organ and no loudspeaker system to relay his sermon. The noise outside became so intense that no one could hear him anymore, so he wound up the service as quickly as propriety would allow. It meant forgoing the usual Christmas collection but it would probably have blown off the plates anyway. The important thing, he thought somewhat sanctimoniously, was that he had managed to get through communion.

The next time the candles fluttered briefly he waved his ringed hand at his wide-eyed flock to indicate they should go home.

'May God bless you and protect you,' he called at the backs of their heads as they hurried out into the darkness. If they heard him, they took no notice.

Clinging together in tight little groups they staggered out into the blinding torrent. There was no chance of talking above the noise of the howling gale as some groped their way to their cars, faces down and fighting to win every step into the wind, while those going in the opposite direction were blown down the street at a run like the tumbling leaves of autumn.

Antonio Paoletti's mother caught his arm and pulled

him to her as the family shuffled forward at the rear of the crowd easing towards the cathedral doors, reaching across one another to dip their fingertips into the font of holy water and make a final sign of the cross.

'Antonio, you come home with us,' she shouted into his ear.

He shook his head and put his arm round her shoulders as the movement of the crowd pressed them together.

'I have to be with my friends, Mamma. They are expecting me.'

'This is a bad night, Antonio. And it is Christmas. You should be with your brothers and sisters.'

They were pushed out into the howling night hunched down with arms up to protect their heads from the viciousness of the rain. He did not see his mother go, for suddenly he was battling to keep his balance, cursing as water flowed into his shoes.

He was almost run down as he crossed the road, and when he found his car he had to force the door open with both hands. Leaning back against it, he lowered the window to reduce the pressure on the door as he struggled into the driver's seat and allowed the door to crash shut behind him.

The main street lights were still on but, with the windscreen wipers unable to cope with the rain, he drove virtually blind along roads awash with water, gripping tightly on to the steering wheel as the car shuddered in the gale. At times, when he changed direction, he stopped to close one window and open the one on the lee side of the car to give him at least some area of vision.

Two police cars went past, heading back to base, but he met no other traffic as he drove slowly towards Fannie Bay. As he neared the house he heard with a shock the crash of metal on the nearside of the car and thought momentarily he had run into another vehicle. Then he saw a sheet of roofing iron flip across the bonnet and whirl away into the darkness like a piece of silver paper. That would have put a nice scrape on his paintwork, he thought bitterly.

He had to park in the street because the drive of the house was packed with a line of cars stretching out from the carport between the concrete pillars supporting the elevated floor of the building.

He clung with both hands to the railings as he climbed the steel staircase to the front door. With breathtaking suddenness his spectacles were snatched from his nose. The cyclone had mounted to a ceaseless roar now, stripping foliage from the trees and picking up the increasing debris to hammer it against walls and windows. He battered the door desperately with his fists, shouting at the top of his voice. Someone must have been close by for it opened quickly and he fell inside to be grabbed in a bear-hug squeeze by a strong pair of arms.

'Tony, baby, what's all the panic? The party's still going.'

Paoletti looked up at a grinning, bearded face.

'Christ, Bazza, it's murder out there. I didn't think I was going to make it.'

'That's the trouble with you spags. You're always so pessimistic,' the big man boomed. 'It's just a bit of a blow, man. Stay cool. And you might as well get out of those clothes. You're as wet as a baby's bum.'

Paoletti was guided firmly down a hallway reeking of marijuana smoke and into a barely furnished bedroom in which about a dozen people were sitting on floor-boards and two mattresses thrown down by the bed. Bazza took no notice of them as he took the Italian up to a rough-looking wardrobe, the only piece of furniture in the room apart from the bed.

'I've got a spare pair of strides here somewhere,' he said, opening the door and sifting through an odd assortment of clothing, male and female.

'Try getting into these.' A pair of trousers hit Paoletti on the chest and he snatched at them quickly to prevent their falling to the floor.

'They won't fit you but you couldn't look worse than you do now. There's a towel in the bathroom.'

Bazza vaguely indicated the direction as he sat down on the bed, pushing aside the legs of the two girls who seemed to have passed out on it.

'Who's got all the grass around here?' he asked.

A good-looking Asian girl, naked from the waist up was posing in front of the bathroom mirror. Paoletti stripped off his clinging wet T-shirt and as he grabbed a towel from the rail in front of her she seemed to notice him for the first time.

'The world is full of beauty and love. Don't you know that?' she smiled. She took her black breasts in her hands, turning slightly as she continued to admire herself.

'Sure it is,' he agreed, vigorously towelling his hair. She was flying high. She picked up the other towel and reached tentatively towards him as though a crevasse had opened up in the floor between them.

'We must care for one another to make it all beautiful,' she assured him. 'I will dry you.'

The wind now was hurling water and debris against the weatherboard walls in a continuous bombardment. He could feel the whole house shuddering in the sudden hammer-blows of the gale, while a constant vibrating roar filled the air as a background to the din, almost like the distant sound of the big jets reversing their engines as they landed at Darwin airport.

Suddenly he felt again the choking grip of fear. The relief of reaching the shelter of the house drained from him as he realised how vulnerable it was, perched on its concrete stilts. Timber, asbestos and iron hanging together on a few nails and bolts. He had helped his father build too many Darwin houses to have confidence in their strength.

'It's Tony!' the girl exclaimed, peering at him through a keyhole in her consciousness. 'Can anyone around here tell me what's going on?'

Paoletti pushed her aside and climbed quickly into the dry trousers.

'Is Marie here?' he asked her.

'Marie?'

'Yeah, Marie. You know, my bird. Is she in the house? Is she at the party?'

The door opened suddenly and Bazza hurried in with an arm round a girl who was holding the side of her face with blood-covered hands.

'My God, what happened?' Paoletti asked.

'Window broke. Glass flying everywhere,' Bazza snapped. 'Have a look in that bloody cabinet there. Should be some medical gear.'

Bazza started bathing the sobbing girl's face and the blood flowed freely down her cheek each time he paused to rinse out the cloth.

'You're a lucky girl,' he told her. 'It just missed your eye.'

He handed Paoletti a box of band aids.

'Take those to the others, will you, Tony? There's a few cuts out there. You'd better get everyone in the kitchen. It's on the safest side of the house.'

Paoletti grabbed the Asian girl by the wrist and pulled her towards the door.

'And ask the girls if any of them is a nurse,' Bazza suggested. 'I could do with some help here.'

Most of the crowd from Bazza's bedroom were standing in the hall outside the bathroom door. They

140

were all soaking wet. Several of them were dabbing cuts on their arms and legs with their handkerchiefs. Paoletti handed the band aids to a girl who was bleeding.

'Everyone into the kitchen.' He shouted to make himself heard above the roaring wind. Water was running like a river from under the bedroom door.

'Man, it was bad in there,' gasped a lean-looking youth who was in the process of wringing his T-shirt out on to the floor. 'When that window blew, it was like being in a whirlpool.'

Paoletti could hear a new sound, a deep creaking noise as though the house itself was straining to break free from its anchorage. He felt water on his head, looked up to see it dripping through the ceiling and started pushing people down the corridor.

Bazza joined them in the kitchen with the weeping girl holding a bloody towel to her face.

'What's the time?' he yelled.

'Quarter to two,' someone replied.

'Turn that radio on, then. There's supposed to be another report coming up.'

The sound of soothing orchestral music came from the transistor.

'What did those warnings tell you to do?' Bazza asked.

'Put away everything that can fly around,' someone suggested.

'Okay, well let's get to it,' Bazza told him. 'Grab those pots and pans and stuff 'em in the cupboards. And all those beer cans.'

One of the girls started reciting: 'Store drinking water in bath tubs . . .'

'Bugger that,' said Bazza. 'What else?'

'Keep a window open on the side away from the wind. Shelter under tables or beds.'

She broke off as sirens blared on the radio.

'Tropical Cyclone Tracy was located by radar at 1.30 a.m. Central Standard Time fourteen miles west-north-east of Darwin moving east-south-east at four miles an hour,' an urgent voice announced.

'God, it's not even here yet!' a girl screamed. 'It will go on for hours!'

Paoletti grabbed Bazza's arm.

'They say the strongest winds are round the eye. The house will never stand it.'

'Listen!' the guy next to them shouted, looking anxiously up the ceiling. 'The roof's being ripped off. I tell you it's coming off!'

'Cool it! Cool it!' Bazza yelled, spreading his arms above the crowd. 'We've got to get organised. Now, open that window like they said and we'll get everything we can find to shelter under into here. There's a big old table in the other room, and there's the mattresses. We better bring 'em all in.'

'Even the ones in the front bedroom? They'll be soaked.' Bazza glared at the speaker. 'It doesn't matter a damn if they're soaked, you idiot! Come and help me get them.

Both of them had to push on the bedroom door to force it open. Fighting against a stinging torrent of water, they wedged a chair in the doorway and crawled into the room on hands and knees to drag out the sodden mattresses. The creaking noise was stronger here, the sound of nails being pulled out of wood. Bazza looked up through a gaping hole in the ceiling and saw the corner of the roof was lifting.

Somehow they got the mattresses back into the kitchen.

'Everyone find a place where they can shelter,' Bazza told them. 'Lie as close as you can to the sink cupboards and drag the mattresses on top of you.'

There was a scramble for places and the sound of

breaking glass. Paoletti was squatting in a pool of water under a table.

He had found Marie with the crowd in the kitchen and now she was trembling in his arms as bodies pressed all round them.

'Some of you get under the bed in the other room,' Bazza shouted. 'There's not room for all of us in here. Hurry up! I'm going to turn the power off.'

The lights of Darwin were going out, one house at a time at first, then in streets and whole sections of suburbs as jagged iron sheets amongst the swirling debris sliced through power lines and steel posts began to bend before the wind and its pounding wreckage.

Paul Rennick was screaming hysterically in the lavatory of his shuddering home. He was standing legs astride pressing his hands against both walls as though he could prevent them falling in to crush him. Why, God, oh why, hadn't he gone to the party? At least he would have died with the others instead of here alone. He was in pitch darkness with water running down the light flex and pouring over him. To his surprise it tasted salty, as though the sea itself was washing over the city. He didn't dare leave the lavatory to see what was happening to the rest of the house.

He did not even have the sound of his transistor to keep him company any longer. The radio station had gone off the air suddenly after the 2.30 a.m. warning that the eye of the cyclone was expected to pass across the city shortly. Panic swept over him as the insane crashing grew louder. What was happening out there? It sounded like an endless artillery bombardment, blanketing the continual thunder. A terrifying, unbearable noise that seemed to clutch him by the throat.

He had tried singing carols. He had tried talking to himself. Now he was screaming.

'Stop it! For God's sake stop it!'

He was going to die. He wished it would be quick. If he lived until the eye came, at least he would be able to look outside. Then the wind would be back, from the opposite direction.

He thought about his friends. He thought about his car. It was under the house, probably a wreck by now. He thought about his parents and how close he had been to going to Sydney with them for Christmas. Suddenly his legs buckled and he was vomiting into the lavatory.

There was a sound like a muffled explosion, close by, then a bigger explosion and the roof was gone. It just took off, timber, ceiling and all, and the night howled above his little box carrying the streaming rain across the top of it so fiercely that only a light spray showered down on him.

On hands and knees, he crawled as tightly as he could under the cistern, curling up into a ball and sobbing with uncontrollable fear, his palms wet with tears.

In terror and in darkness, Darwin was being raked by the whims of a savage giant. The weather bureau's anemograph at the airport recorded a gust of 136 m.p.h. at 3.05 a.m. before the city's power supply failed completely and the telemetry link in the recording system was cut. As windows and doors blew out, fragile houses exploded, walls and roofs spinning away into the night. Others disintegrated slowly, torn away piece by piece while families ran from room to room, huddling together to combine their weight, crawling into wardrobes, hanging on to sink pipes and baths and lavatories to prevent themselves being blown away along with their possessions.

From the harbourmaster's office Bob Jordan stared in disbelief as loaded twenty-ton containers skidded across the wharf and plunged into the boiling sea. When the lights failed, he had managed to struggle along the wall of the container shed to his car to switch on its head-lights so that he could see at least something of what was happening. Now the car was on its roof, the lights still glowing to illuminate the chaos.

As if locked in his own nightmare, he saw steel girders lifted from the top of the stack on the wharf and flipped away like swirling straws. The great weighted hooks hanging on the crane cables were suddenly fishermen's lines flying in the offshore breeze.

Through the darkness he could just make out two of the naval patrol boats bucking at their cyclone moorings. There were dozens of ocean-going yachts in harbour and about thirty larger vessels. The others had put to sea as the cyclone approached in the hope of riding it out, God help them. He had seen three groups of distress flares between midnight and 1 a.m. The phones were already out. There was nothing he could do, nothing anyone could do. In universal terror, everyone was alone.

The fear that was gnawing Jordan's guts was not for himself but for Kay and the children. How were they making out? Was the house still standing? Were they all dead, or pinned broken and bleeding beneath the wreckage? God, Kay was frightened of a thunderstorm. Alone in this terror she would be demented, convinced that he had died somewhere out in the night when he didn't get home by 1 a.m.

In his agony of mind he could see the house, its brittle walls punctured by airborne debris, its timbers battered into matchwood. Flying girders! What chance did they have? And so terribly alone. He smashed his fists on the table and screamed out his frustration and helplessness. Suddenly he realised he was praying, and he knew what prayer was all about. It was for others.

By 3.30 a.m. explosive gusts of more than 160 m.p.h. were tearing the city apart. Now brick walls were disintegrating. Concrete pylons snapped like pretzel sticks, and tall buildings swayed. Sturdy, modern blocks of flats tumbled into their gardens, and historic stone structures that had stood for more than a hundred years began to break up.

The Taylor family was scattered in the wreckage of its home. Only one of the walls was still clinging to the platform floor. It was leaning across the bath in which Bev Taylor was lying semi-conscious but still clasping the baby in her bleeding arms. Her husband was on the floor beside her, clinging with both hands to one foot of the bath with his ankles locked round the other. The interior walls had gone, sweeping most of the furniture away with them. He could just make out the kitchen sink unit standing on the edge of the platform. There was no way of seeing if the old lady was still huddled under it. He didn't know where the boys were. When the roof had been ripped off he was too busy getting Bev and the baby to the bathroom to see where they had gone. They were probably under the pile of wreckage still held in place where their bedroom had once been by the fallen roof timbers. Maybe dead.

It seemed long ago they had all been together picking out their presents from under the Christmas tree. Trying to laugh away the mounting din around them. It was taking so long to die. There was no other way out of this hell.

At last the end was here. He felt the floor lifting beneath him in the final sledgehammer blast. The broken timbers flew. The wall gone. The remaining debris swept away. The sink unit tore free. It crashed to the ground. He struggled to his feet to die.

The old lady found herself in the garden, face down in muddy water. Had she been unconscious? There was no pain. No reality. She crawled across the ground. Behind a sheet of iron clamped against the big tree she started to dig a hole for herself in the mud. Then the wind stopped. It moved away down the street like a rattling freight train. No rain. Breathless silence.

Chapter Twelve

Out of the eerie hush grew the sounds of the anguish of a dying city.

It started with dogs barking, their distant howls echoing across the black stillness of the night. Then came the human cries, a stirring in the wreckage. Calls for help, screams of pain, the shouting of a thousand names as families searched the endless debris for the missing and the dead.

Some still had torches, trembling patches of yellow light that flickered across the littered ground, returning it to darkness when the sweeping pools of vision ran up and along the timber skeletons of broken houses.

Some still had car keys, so they concentrated first on pulling the wreckage clear of the cars so that they could be moved into position to illuminate the search with their headlights.

Most simply groped in the darkness for the injured, crawling in the mud and water under fallen sections of wall and roof as others lifted them, feeling about blindly. And when the buried were found, when the battered, bloody figures were drawn quietly unconscious or crying in agony from beneath the debris, few families had any medical supplies left to tend to their wounds. So they did what they could, laying out the dead and bathing the injured often in the only water available, which was still flowing fast along the streets.

Some worked, others prayed. As families, together again in a blessed calm, they fell to their knees amongst the ruins of their homes, thinking their ordeal was over, believing divine intervention had saved their lives, thanking God in a dozen languages for the gift of survival.

Few understood they were in the eye of the cyclone and round them all a whirling circular wall of water towered in the black night, moving steadily across the shattered suburbs.

Alex Taylor knew about the eye. He did not know how he was still alive or how much time he had to search before the inner wall of the cyclone hit again, its vicious blows delivered this time from the opposite direction.

He moved automatically, not thinking about what he was doing, the pain of his own bruised and lacerated body numbed by inner grief. He had got Bev and the baby into the car with the old lady. The windows were broken but it was the only shelter left. He had given the women strict instructions to stay there while he looked for the boys.

The limp corpse of his younger son was in his arms as he stepped carefully through strewn timber and iron, pausing occasionally to work out a path or simply to lower his head and hug the boy closely to him. He cut a length off the clothes-line with a wedge of broken glass he found beneath the house and tied the boy's body face inwards and upright tightly against one of the round steel pillars supporting the floor platform.

As he returned to search for his other son his foot struck a large saucepan sending it clattering across a sheet of iron. He took it to the street to fill with water for them to drink in the car. A woman almost knocked him over as he bent to dip the saucepan into the gutter flow.

'My baby! Dear God, have you seen my baby?'

She stared at him wild-eyed as he stood up, shaking him hysterically by the shoulders.

'She blew out of my arms,' she screamed. 'She just blew out of my arms!'

He grabbed her, pinning her arms to her sides.

'You must get back. How far have you come?'

She struggled as he held her, shaking her head violently.

'There is nothing you can do,' he shouted. 'You must get back.'

A man approached from the darkness.

'Can I help?' he asked Taylor. 'We still have a roof on.'

'Take her.' He thrust the woman towards him.

'Have you any injured? We have bandages, just a few.'

Taylor shook his head. 'Take her,' he repeated, walking away.

There were too many people out in the open, too many just wandering about. He heard the sound of hammering. Some idiot was up on his roof, nailing it back down.

Hammers all over the city. Bang, bang, bang. He could hear their pounding growing in the distance. Louder and louder, swelling to a staccato rattle. Had they all gone mad? Nearer and nearer. He clasped his hands to his ears and screamed.

'Get off the roof! Get off the roof!'

And for Alex Taylor the returning roar of the cyclone became the roar of approaching eternity.

Chapter Thirteen

Howling gale. Blinding rain. Lightning. Thunder. With devastating suddenness, the peak ferocity of Tracy returned. Now steel bent. Twisted. Walls leaning inward were snatched away by the reversed direction of the onslaught. Cars rolled in the streets. Concrete buildings shuddered.

Too many people in the open. Scything sheets of iron. Spears of iron and timber. Bodies hurled through the air.

Alex Taylor's boy regained consciousness as the wind lifted the wreckage from on top of him and water slapped his face. Instinctively he started crawling, dragging his right leg across the sodden lawn. He feared he would faint from the pain. Something heavy thumped the ground beside him and bounced past. He got the impression it was a bath. Ahead, slightly to his left, he could just make out a dark outline. He struggled towards it, hoping it would offer some shelter. The car! He recognised it as he reached the house pillars, resting against one for a moment to gather his strength for the final effort to reach it. What did the coach tell the school football team? You are never beaten until you give up?

Suddenly he had to get away from the pillars. Had to cross the last stretch of open ground. A few painful, terrifying yards and his cheek was pressed against the cold wet steel of the mudguard. He reached up for the door handle. Perhaps it would open. Perhaps he could crawl inside.

Strong hands were helping him. The pain from his

leg came screaming from his throat, and then he was sobbing in his grandmother's arms.

'Michael, Michael!' His mother reached across the back of the front seat to stroke his forehead, gulping down her emotion, wanting to say much more. The car rocked violently.

'Your father? Did you see your father?'

The boy shook his head, staring up at the ceiling light she had switched on.

'And what about Grant? Did you see Grant?'

He nodded, and the tears welled from his eyes.

'Are we all going to die, Mum?'

The sight of his brother's body, hanging limply against the pillar, was imprinted on his mind. He could not tell her for a long time.

And while he cried, as they comforted him, debris piled up against the windward side of the car, jammed against it by the strength of the gale, to form a solid, protective shield against Tracy's bombardment.

As the last, strongest houses were torn apart, it was better to be buried under the wreckage on the ground than trying to shelter in the swaying, disintegrating remains. So the injured, the survivors, clung thankfully to the wet earth waiting for the eternal night to end and dawn to bring perspective to their nightmare.

Only a few of the larger vessels remained afloat in the harbour, bucking and tugging at their anchor chains like wild stallions trying to shake free of their halters. The dinghies and ocean yachts had been wiped from the foaming surface early in the onslaught. Many cracked open like eggshells as they smashed together or against the wharf piles after being torn from their moorings. Others carried for miles to be thrown as splintered wrecks on distant beaches.

Lieutenant Neville Jackson was fighting a losing battle to keep H.M.A.S. *Venom* afloat. He had given up thinking about the possibility of slipping her cyclone mooring. Now the stocky little patrol boat was dragging a six-ton anchorage steadily across the bottom of the harbour, edging all the time closer to shore.

Jackson was young and inexperienced. He had commanded the *Venom* for only four months, cutting his teeth on one of the navy's popular little 'Bathtub Babies' as they were known throughout the service, in preparation for bigger things to come.

They were fun first commands. After three years at naval college and two as a junior officer on a good-will-tripping destroyer, he was enjoying command and the eventfulness of the constant northern patrols. True, he was only picking up scraggy-looking Asian fishermen poaching in territorial waters and a few long-haired layabouts trying to sail in a bit of pot from Bali, but it was a job to do and it had to be done properly. Australia's front line of defence! So *Venom* would close in on her unarmed prey with a flak-suited gunner crouching behind her 40 mm forward machine-gun and a boarding party of six, armed with pistol and sub-machine-guns ready to jump aboard as soon as she came alongside. It was the procedure laid down. Jackson's one frustration was that he had never been given the opportunity to fire a warning shot across a bow. He had been tempted at times, but he always went by the book.

He was going by the book now, and it wasn't working. It didn't cater for this kind of situation. Christ, the navy had never experienced this kind of situation before! Here they were in port and the wind was stripping the paintwork back to bare steel while all round them ships were sinking. The radio was alive with distress calls, barely audible above the din. The three big ferries had gone to the bottom, one of the tugs had sunk after being smashed against a wharf, and a couple of prawn trawlers which had sailed out to meet the cyclone had gone off the air after reporting their steering had gone and waves were smashing over the wheelhouse.

Still, the best bet was to get out of harbour, to ride it out at sea. How the hell had the *Vixen* managed to slip her mooring and get away while he was sitting here with a noose around his neck like a lamb awaiting the slaughterer? He had tried everything he knew to get enough slack in the mooring chain to release the shackle, but *Venom* refused to close up to the buoy. Then both engines had overheated, his petty officer had been blown over the bow rails and that was the end of that. God only knows how they managed to pull him back on board.

Now *Vixen* was out to sea with a fighting chance while he was locked to a mooring that was dragging despite the fact that he had both engines running at three-quarter speed to try to take the strain off the chain.

Their sister ship, H.M.A.S. *Viper*, was already aground, swept into shore like a piece of flotsam when her mooring chain shredded as though it were rotten rope.

Three times *Venom* had been struck by drifting dinghies while Jackson gritted his teeth and wished for the first time since his promotion that he was back with the fleet waiting for someone else to make the decisions.

'Damn it, I've got to give her more revs!' he yelled to his sub-lieutenant.

'She'll seize,' Bob Graves replied. 'The screws are coming clean out of the water. She'll over-rev.'

Jackson pushed both handles on the engine-room telegraph forward to full ahead.

'I've got eighteen lives in my hands. We've got to try to hold her. We're already too damn close to shore.'

His arm felt as though it was about to be ripped from his shoulder as he hung on grimly to the ceiling rail.

For six hours he and Graves had been bounced about the little cabin like balls in a pinball machine. He was bruised and aching, mentally exhausted through tension and lack of sleep and physically drained by the constant effort of bracing himself against the bucking floor. It felt as though someone had spent the night kicking his knees.

Yes, he had to take the gamble. He could always reduce revs if the warning light came on, and meanwhile he was buying them time. More than an hour had passed since the lull in which the *Vixen* had unshackled. That meant the eye had passed and the cyclone was decreasing even though it did not seem like it. He wished his radar was still operating so that he could check its rate of movement.

He did not see the windlass disintegrating. The roar of the cyclone drowned the sound of tearing steel as the straining mooring chain ripped it out of the deck.

'We've broken loose,' he shouted as the bow swung and he felt the strain on the wheel.

Almost immediately the engine temperature warning buzzer sounded and a red light flashed on the control panel. He cut the revs and held her head into the wind.

'We've got nothing left,' he told Graves. 'I'm going to let her drift back until we are close to the wharf and then try to bring her alongside. If I give her everything she's got we may be able to hold her long enough for the crew to get ashore.'

'You're abandoning?'

'She's going to go down or aground anyway,' he snapped. 'It's the best chance for the crew. Now, get them organised.' He started flicking switches on the lighting panel, turning on the forward searchlight, the deck floods, every light he had.

He could see the outline of the wharf leaping wildly

against the sky. Wait, wait. It kept on slipping past. He had to time it right. A forty-four-gallon drum of diesel fuel came spinning over the edge, dropping into the sea alongside the *Venom*.

Now! He gunned the engines to full ahead and the bucking ship moved sideways towards the pylons. Graves was leaning out of the cabin door watching for the ladders along the curving wharf. The warning light was still glowing red. She could only be a few minutes from seizing.

The first crew members were jumping for the ladders. A couple were shinning up the wooden piles. Jackson could see them now through *Venom*'s round spin-clear windows as she started to slip backwards. They were lit by the swinging searchlight like frantic actors in some crazy play. One of the men lost his grip on a pile and fell backwards into the sea. Jackson watched in horror, helpless, as the first sailor reached the top of the ladder only to be struck by one of the bouncing diesel drums as he tried to clamber on to the wharf. His body dropped like a limp doll and disappeared in the raging water.

Suddenly there was a bone-shaking crash as *Venom* was smashed against one of the piles. Timber and concrete rained on the deck as the wharf supports gave way. Jackson shut down the engines and raced for the side. Looking up, he could see railway line hanging bent across a gaping hole in the wharf above him. The crew had gone. There was no sign of Graves.

The *Venom* was listing heavily to starboard and sinking at the stern. With desperate, fumbling hands he unlashed a life raft and tossed it over the side. Almost as it hit the water, he jumped after it.

The lights of Bob Jordan's overturned car still illuminated the top of the wharf. From his office he saw a section of it sag then break away as the *Venom* struck.

He ran out with the idea of throwing some lifebelts but was immediately bowled over by the wind and just managed to save himself from being flung over the edge by grabbing the base of a bent lighting pole. As the survivors came over the top he scrambled with them back to the office, grateful at last no longer to be alone.

Trapped in the fractured remains of his suburban home, young Paul Rennick was still on his own. His hopes of finding some company by making a run for one of the neighbouring houses during the lull of the eye disappeared when the swaying walls of the lavatory ripped open like paper sheets, showering him with timber and plaster. He could move the rest of his body but something heavy was pinning down his leg. The precious lull came and went. There was a numbness and warm waves of unconsciousness sweeping up his body to black out his mind and shut off the renewed roar of the cyclone. The bleeding from his head had stopped. That had been the worst thing, the blood running and running and his not knowing how to stop it. At first he had used wet toilet paper. Then he had taken off his pyjama jacket and torn it into strips to bind over the wound. He was drenched with salty water, and bitterly cold but no longer afraid. When he surfaced to consciousness for a while his own calmness surprised him. The cyclone was still there, as fierce and terrifying in the darkness as ever, but now he seemed immune to it. There was nothing he could do, no decisions he had to make.

In the long moments of clarity he thought about his life critically, dispassionate as a stranger. What had he done with twenty-two years? Precious little, for life was all ahead of him. How confident he had been of that. 'The future is yours,' his father used to say. How could anyone say that? Now it seemed so amusing. He had been planning a joke on himself. All that he had to show for his life had been blown away.

159

He wondered how he would start again in the morning if he was still alive. No food, no clothes, no water, no home, no money. He smiled to himself as the faintness returned and he felt himself floating, his mind riding away on the winds of the cyclone.

As Tracy's eye moved steadily away to the south-east and its final fury lashed the devastated city, houses which had withstood the onslaught for hours gradually fell apart. Walls which had stayed in place long after the roof had gone now leaned slowly outwards, toppling one at a time into the garden. The scouring rain gnawed the mortar from between the bricks to loosen walls and pillars, weakening them so that they collapsed before the fading winds.

Somehow the end section of roof was still clinging to the beams of the house at Fannie Bay.

Paoletti scrambled out from beneath the mattress and stretched his aching limbs. He felt the snap of glass breaking on the kitchen floor beneath his feet.

'How much longer can this thing go on?' he asked wearily.

It was the first time any of them had spoken since the eye passed over them. There had been an argument about whether it was better to stay where they were or to seek some safer shelter. A few had gone out into the night, but most of them decided it was wiser to remain, for at least they had some cover.

'It'll be dawn soon,' said someone.

Paoletti pushed some fallen ceiling plaster aside with his foot and gingerly opened the kitchen door, taking the pressure as it was forced towards him.

'I'm going to take a look around.'

Water sprayed on his face as he stepped into the hallway. The front door had disappeared, in fact it looked as though the entire outside wall had gone. The top half of the inside wall had broken away and he could see the roofing timbers naked against the sky. The whole building was still shuddering and creaking, its remaining walls rattling like machine-guns in the hail of storm shrapnel.

He pushed open the door of the first bedroom and peered into the darkness.

'Where's Bazza?' he shouted.

'He's asleep,' replied a voice from somewhere on his right.

'Asleep! My God!' Paoletti groped his way into the room until he bumped against the bed. He felt a large form stretched out on the bedsprings, grabbed a shoulder and shook it. 'He, Bazza! Wake up!'

'Get off me, will you?' Bazza shrugged away the Italian's hand and rolled over on to his side.

Paoletti shook him again.

'He doesn't understand,' Bazza muttered to himself. '*Arrivederci! Arrivederci!*' he roared, giving Paoletti a shove.

'The place is falling to bits,' Paoletti persisted. 'Half the roof's gone and the walls are swaying. You'd better come and take a look.'

Complaining loudly, the big man swung his feet to the floor.

'What the hell do you want me to do about it?'

He staggered to the door and looked out into the hallway.

'Christ, what a party! I'm glad I'm only renting this place.'

He pulled Paoletti out of the bedroom and yelled to the others inside.

'We'd better all get in the kitchen. This pad's getting torn apart room by room, and this one will be next.'

As he spoke another section of wall split and tore away with the sound of breaking timber. The two of them ducked as they were showered with plaster from the disintegrating ceiling. There was a rush from the bedroom to the kitchen.

Bazza found a torch and shone it round the room. There were twenty people in there, huddled together under the tables and mattresses, looking up with frightened faces at the sudden glare of the light. Rain was spraying in a shattered window on one side of the room and water was streaming down the inside of the rear wall.

'It can't take much more of this,' said Paoletti. 'The whole place is going to go.'

Suddenly Marie struggled free from the bodies pressing against her under the table and made a dash for the door.

'We're all going to die! We've got to get out of here!' she screamed.

Paoletti made a grab for her as her hand reached the handle of the door. It swung open viciously, knocking them both to the floor with Marie still screaming hysterically. He flung himself across her body, seizing her wrists and pinning them back above her head as she fought violently to get free. Bazza rushed across to help him as the last sections of the roof were ripped from above them.

'There's nowhere to go,' he yelled at her. She was spluttering and twisting her head as the rain lashed her face.

'We all stay here, together,' said Paoletti. 'Just hang on, Marie. Hang on.'

Between them they half carried and half dragged her back across the kitchen and stretched her out on the floor beneath the stove, Paoletti lay down beside her, taking her in his arms while she sobbed uncontrollably.

'It won't last much longer, darling,' he told her. 'The wind is not as bad as it was.'

'I'm so scared, Tony,' she gasped through her tears.

He tightened his grip on her as beams of timber started falling around them.

'I wonder what's happened to my family,' he said.

The rumbling roar of Tracy receded with the night, its final power absorbed in the timbered wilderness of the bush as it moved towards the lightening eastern skies.

The wind was still driving the rain at gale force as Bishop Madigan and Father Miller hurried, heads down, across the sparse lawn of Bishop's House on their way to the cathedral. They had spent the night sitting in opposite corners of a shower recess with water pouring over them as the roof was demolished over their heads.

Through the night the Bishop had been fretting with anxiety about the cathedral. He wished they had stayed there instead of coming home after Mass. They would probably have been drier and safer if they had, and he would have been able to keep an eye on things. In the din and the darkness he could not push from his mind visions of sheets of iron and debris swirling about inside the building, smashing into the pulpit and font, gouging great chunks from those beautiful carvings. Maybe even the altar itself had been damaged! And what about the stained-glass window of Our Lady Star of the Sea? It was a feature of the building and quite priceless, for it could never be replaced.

The wreckage and pools of water were slowing their progress, and several times the Bishop's feet nearly slipped from under him as he stepped across piles of smashed asbestos, iron and timber. He paused for a moment, wiping his long white hair back from his forehead, as he craned to work out the best route to the cathedral door. He could see a sheet of iron wrapped round the cross on top of the bell tower.

'This way, My Lord, I think,' the young priest volunteered. The Bishop hurried on, picking his way through the mud which was splashing progressively higher up his black trousers.

The big old gum tree from which the birds used to call to him as he walked in morning prayer stood stark against the pale sky, its great branches gone, a jagged stump. The lush tropical foliage which once hid the gardens from the street had all been stripped away so that now through a row of bare, black trunks he could see the city buildings looming on the skyline. There was no colour anywhere.

He stopped suddenly, gripping the priest by the arm.

'Oh! Do look at that!'

The life-size statue of the Madonna had lost its head and stood forlornly chipped and scarred above the debris gathered around its pedestal.

'She has stood there for more than fifty years,' the Bishop said dejectedly.

With the priest close behind him, he opened the side door of the cathedral slowly. There was water on the stone floor and debris beneath two gaping holes that had been punched through the transept walls but no sign of any severe damage to the internal fittings.

'The roof has held very well,' the priest assured him. 'There are only a few sections missing.'

Footsteps echoing, they walked down beside the high altar and across the front of the nave, genuflecting in the centre before entering the altar rails. The Bishop gave a grateful sigh of relief. There was no debris near the altar and no sign of damage that he could see in the half-light. Almost every window was shattered but, miraculously, the precious stained glass was still intact.

'Praise be to God,' he murmured.

He heard the sound of movement in the nave behind then and turned to see a head emerging from one of the front pews.

'Who's that there?' he called.

'It's me, Father. Mrs Mazzone.'

He moved towards her curiously. 'What are you doing here, Mrs Mazzone?'

More heads appeared gradually from beneath the pews and a child began crying as a dozen voices started talking at once. The Bishop raised his hands to quieten them as he looked around the frightened, bedraggled figures in complete surprise. There must have been forty of them at least, not counting the babies.

'Mrs Mazzone, you tell me,' he said. 'I can't listen to you all at once.'

'Our homes have been blown away, Father. Everything has gone. So when the storm was quiet for a while in the middle of the night we all ran here. It was the only place we had to go.'

The Bishop walked slowly along the ends of the pews, his hand to his chin as he looked at the family groups, the mothers with children on their laps, the elderly sitting quietly and others still stretched out on the floor beneath the seats.

'Are any of you hurt?' he asked.

'This man here has hurt his leg,' replied a lad whose face was familiar to him. He tried to recall the name. 'A piece of glass has gone right into it.'

'My head was bleeding, Father, but it's stopped now,' a woman called out.

The light was getting stronger and he could see there were only a few pieces of debris scattered about inside the building. His fears had been for nothing.

'There's a first-aid box in the vestry, Father Miller. Would you mind getting it please?' he said. 'We must look after the injured first, and then we will see if we can get you all a nice hot cup of tea and some sort of breakfast. We'll have to use the gas barbecues we take on the picnics.'

He was standing at the side door, staring out into the

streaming rain as Father Miller came back from the vestry. The priest stopped behind him as though expecting further instructions.

"It's Christmas morning,' said the Bishop without looking round. 'Do you think they will be coming to the seven-thirty Mass?'

The clouds hid the sunrise that revealed the devastation.

As the last winds faded, the manager of the Buffalo Motel was checking the rooms, picking up the doors that had blown into the corridors and propping them against the walls. Every window was broken, every room saturated with water, its fittings and furnishing smashed and overturned. The guests had spent a sleepless night crowded together in the dining-room where the only damage had been the loss of a few panels from the suspended ceiling.

He found a gruesome corpse in a room on the sixth floor. The head had been almost severed from the body which was propped up in a corner with glass embedded in the clothing. He did not see it until he was in the room and turned round to find the vacant, startled eyes staring at him.

Shocked, he walked out on to the balcony and leaned over the rail to gaze down at the motel's naked garden and the tops of two cars which had blown from the car park into the swimming pool

With growing incredulity he slowly raised his eyes to stare in horror at a dead, devastated city as the rain faded to a mist and over the grey panorama of tragic ruins settled an unbelievable, blessed hush.

Chapter Fourteen

Ray Mead stirred slowly beneath the wreckage. In the final, waning hours of the cyclone, sleep had snatched at him as he lay on the sodden earth at the foot of a low stone garden wall. During the times he dozed he seemed to stay conscious of the noise and the wet so that when he awoke it came as a surprise to find he had been asleep. The silence was uncanny, and there was sunshine.

The door he had crawled under for protection from the rain and flying debris was still on top of him. He pushed it upwards with his elbow and it toppled over to crash noisily on to a sheet of iron.

Mead stood up cautiously, suspicious of the stillness and the state of his own body. Unconsciously, he checked himself over, running his hands over his body, stretching and flexing his joints and muscles as he stared in utter disbelief at the scene around him.

He was surrounded by total devastation. Where yesterday there had been a green gardened suburb, not a house was left standing. Within a terrible bleak horizon homes had been smashed to pulp as though some giant fist had descended on them leaving the remains strewn across the floor platforms and hanging from them in frozen cascades of timber and wallboard. The lush tropical greenness had gone, the trees stripped bare of leaves, bark and branches to be left as ugly tapered stakes, and the plants which once had filled the gardens with colour carried away by the wind or buried beneath the ground mantle of wreckage. Sprinkled through the chaos were the saturated, dead bodies of the birds.

It was as though he were standing in the centre of a vast rubbish dump, for there was personal, domestic litter scattered amongst the twisted iron and broken beams. A man's shoe, a washing-machine on its back, a table lamp, a handbag, clothing, curtains, books. In the distance he could see a complete kitchen sink unit, while close to his feet a new teddy-bear with a gay red ribbon round its neck lay in a pool of water staring blankly up at him with bright button eyes.

He was able to locate the street by the crazy lurching line of electricity poles marking its course as trees trace the submerged banks of a river in flood. Power lines trailed to the ground and sheets of roofing iron were wrapped around the leaning pylons as though they were flimsy pieces of silver paper.

Mead heard a noise behind him and turned round to see that one of the houses still had a wall standing. It was leaning precariously outwards, looking as though the slightest puff of wind would send it toppling into the garden below. A sheet of iron was swinging slightly in the breeze below it, tapping occasionally against one of the steel floor pillars.

There was no other movement, no other sound. It already seemed a miracle to Mead that he was unhurt apart from a few scratches and bruises. Last night he was in gaol. Now he was free. It was all unreal. Was he the only one left alive in this whole city? The thought hit him—had he survived to be trapped in a graveyard? As he stared at the scene again, one word kept going through his mind. Hiroshima. Hiroshima.

He started to pick his way through the wreckage towards the street and as soon as he came out from between the houses he saw with relief about twenty people moving about the remains of a building some hundred yards or so down the road. At least someone else was still alive. As he approached them, carefully stepping across the broken glass and jagged iron littering the roadway, four men combined their strength to lift clear a wall which had fallen inwards. With a joint heave they sent it crashing to the ground below. He saw one of them pull back the covers of a bed which had been pinned under the wall and lift out the body of a young child. A colourful pile of Christmas presents was still at the foot of the bed.

Mead did not stop. What he had to do was find Karen and get the hell out of this place.

There were people everywhere now, sifting through the wreckage, pulling the debris from their cars, cooking breakfasts over wood fires and just sitting staring at the ruins. A man wrapped in a grey blanket came towards him pushing a wheelbarrow containing the blood-spattered figure of a young woman in a pink nightdress. Every now and then he had to turn to drag the barrow backwards across a fallen power-pole or a pile of debris blocking the road. The woman's legs were lolling limply over the front of the barrow, one on either side of the wheel. She appeared to be unconscious.

'A doctor lives around here somewhere,' the man said to the truckie as he passed, as if he needed to explain what he was doing.

As Mead made his way slowly through the chaotic streets, mounting disbelief and shock weakened his resolve until he was wandering almost aimlessly between rows of shattered houses. Nothing was recognisable as street signs had been torn away and all the landmarks had gone; the distinctive houses and gardens used unconsciously in the past to navigate the surburban sea. The new landmarks were the overturned cars that littered the roads. He knew he must be within a mile of the gaol, for the lull had lasted only about twenty minutes after he had made a run from the smashed remains of the remand prisoners' dormitory hut. That meant he was about three miles from Karen's flat, and the city centre was due south. If he kept the sun on his left he would be heading in the general direction. He stepped across a steel light-pole bent horizontal from its base so that the fluorescent head almost touched the ground. He was wondering how long it was going to take him to work his way out of the maze when he spotted the racecourse, a roofless grandstand floating on a sea of water. The track rails, made of white-painted waterpipe, were flattened in some sections and bent and arched in others so that they careered round the course like a crazy switchback. He was surprised to come across it. It was not in a recognisable location, even though some of the houses here had walls still standing. At least now he knew his way to the Stuart Highway and from there it should not take him long to reach the city.

Few people were moving on the streets. As he passed by he could see families huddled under the floors of their homes peering out at him from between the pillars. It seemed that they were waiting for someone to come to help them, to tell them what to do. Mead thought that they might at least have had the sense to start clearing the streets so that some rescue traffic could get through.

Something ahead of him caught his eye. He thought at first it was a piece of iron wrapped around the top of an electricity pole but as he got closer he saw that it was a man's corpse draped across the power lines some fifty feet above the street. He stared up at it incredulously as he walked until a timber beam in the road trapped him and turned his attention back to negotiating a route through the wreckage.

He stopped at a row of half a dozen shattered shops. The door had been blown off the delicatessen so he walked in and helped himself to a couple of cans of soft drink. They were still quite cool when he took them from the lifeless refrigeration cabinet and he drank the first gratefully as he clambered back out across the rubble of bricks and plaster that had tumbled from the single-storey flats above. There was no sign of the occupants, but their possessions were strewn along the pavements.

The damage seemed to be getting less severe as he neared the main road. One house even had its roof still on, standing inexplicably intact amongst the broken remains of its neighbours. As he walked, the varying amount of damage to the buildings recorded the process of destruction like the still frames from a movie. He could see how the houses fell apart. First the roof lifted. Then a wall blew out, taking with it most of the furnishings and freeing the ends of the ceiling joists so that they too ripped away. The remaining walls went quickly after that until finally the whole platform was swept clean as though a knife had sliced across the floorboards.

He lost his way again. He must be somewhere near the highway, but there were no reference points left. He stopped to search the sea of debris ahead for the traffic lights at the intersection. Everything was so still. There was no traffic moving to mark the way to the city.

He cursed as he grazed his shin on a piece of iron. Then he saw the traffic signals, some pointing uselessly skywards, others to the ground, on bent and twisted poles.

He was shocked, tired and hungry, walking through a nightmare world. He passed a used-car yard with rows of wrecked cars, windscreens shattered, some virtually buried beneath debris. Floodlight standards lay across those outside, and the roof had collapsed on top of the cars in the showroom.

Mead felt a surge of relief as tall city buildings came into view. At least they were still standing! He was more hopeful now that Karen was alive and he would be able to find her. The damage was not as bad here as in the suburbs. Roofs had still been blown away but the more modern buildings had managed to withstand the cyclonic winds and give some protection to the older houses between them.

A dented, windowless police car was working its way out from the city centre, stopping every few yards while the occupants got out to drag clear the biggest obstacles. Mead assumed they were police officers, for there was no way of telling from their appearance. They were wearing beach shirts, old pairs of shorts and rubber thongs on their feet.

He kept walking towards them. They were too busy to notice some insignificant prison escapee.

The driver shouted out to him as he got level with them.

'We're trying to get to the hospital. Have you come from that way?'

Mead shook his head and strolled across to the car.

'No, I've just come along the highway. You'll need a bulldozer to clear that.'

The cop offered him a cigarette with a bloody, bandaged hand.

'All communications are out,' he said. 'Tell everybody you see to start clearing the streets. We've got to get the ambulances moving. God knows if we've still got a hospital.'

Mead moved on towards the city centre, quickening his pace as he followed the path through the wreckage cleared by the police car.

There was little sign of life as he walked between footpaths covered with the broken glass of shop windows. Neon signs were hanging limply by their wiring from the pavement verandah ceilings, shop doors had been torn from their hinges, and whole sections of verandah roof sagged above the pavement under the weight of debris piled on top.

Refugees had moved into shops and offices which still offered cover, probably families from the de-roofed flats above. Most of them were in their nightclothes. Bedraggled adults and children were sitting on the floor of one of the banks eating the contents of some cans by tipping them out into their hands.

A small crowd had gathered outside the doors of the supermarket on the corner of Karen's street. As Mead got closer he saw that a tall, grey-haired man, presumably the manager, was handing out dozens of frozen chickens and packets of frozen food which he had wheeled out from the store on a hand trolley. He held up one of the birds towards Mead as he passed.

'Do you want a chook? They're thawing out fast and we'll only have to throw the lot away if they don't get eaten.'

Mead shook his head and looked anxiously down the street towards Karen's flat.

A car was on its side across the kerb outside the gate, its rusty underside displayed as it dripped black oil on to the pavement.

He had to step across a fallen palm tree to get into the courtyard. The garden was a chaotic mess of broken trees and uprooted bushes but the four flats were still standing. The taller rows of shops on either side had probably given them some shelter.

The flat was full of people he did not know. Some were sleeping or dozing restlessly on the chairs, the settee and even the floor in the lounge. He went through to the kitchen and saw that a fire had been lit in the back garden. Two women wrapped in dressing-gowns were squatting beside it holding frying-pans over the flames.

In a corner a man was digging out a latrine with a garden spade. Half of Karen's bedroom ceiling had collapsed and the room was saturated. He could not find her anywhere.

Wearily Mead returned to the kitchen and leaned over the sink, reaching for the tap.

'There's no water, mate,' said a voice behind him. 'That's why I've been digging a hole down the end of the garden.'

Mead turned round, wiping the sweat from his forehead.

'Do you know where Karen is?'

'Who?'

'Karen. The girl who lives here.'

The man looked puzzled for a moment, then his face lit up.

'Was that the good-looking bird? Long blonde hair. Big . . . er . . .' The verbal description faded out as his hands took over the task.

Mead nodded. 'Yes. Where did she go?'

'Oh, they went off . . . must be about half an hour ago. No idea where they went.'

Mead stared at him curiously.

'They? What do you mean, "They"?'

'Well, the big bloke with her. I took it he was the boyfriend.' He glanced at Mead anxiously. 'I don't know, mind you. That's just the way I read it.'

Mead could feel a knot tightening in his stomach.

'What did this guy look like? He was big, you say?'

The latrine digger fidgeted uneasily. He was wishing he had not opened his big mouth in the first place.

'Yeah, yeah. He was well over six foot, fair hair and he didn't dress like a local. He was smart, you know? He was actually wearing a suit when he left here this morning.' He paused. 'And he had a ring on, with a big green stone.' He placed an imaginary ring on the fourth finger of his left hand. 'I remember that. I thought he was a bit of a showman.'

Collins! A stream of confused thought tumbled through Mead's mind. What the hell was that hood doing here with Karen? How had he come to find her? Where had he taken her?

'Was he pushing her around? Did it look as though he was forcing her to leave?'

The man quickly suppressed a nervous laugh.

'Are you kidding? I told you. They were friendly. I thought he was staying here.'

'Do you mean he was here all night?'

'Well, most of the crowd got here about three-thirty, I reckon, and he was here then.'

Mead turned away. He felt sick, nauseated by the sudden surge of uncertainty that was going through him. It had always been his fear that Karen would play around when he wasn't in town. He knew how hot she was, and there were plenty of big spenders among the customers at the club who fancied their chances. He had gone through vivid torments of jealousy at times on the track.

'You look a bit shaken up, mate,' said the latrine digger. 'Have a cup of coffee. The girls are just brewing one up.'

They walked out into the garden and one of the women handed him a steaming mug.

'Made from the finest rainwater,' she told him with a smile.

He sat with the others at the patio table, ignoring their conversation, wrapped in his own thoughts.

Perhaps she had bumped into Collins again at the club. Perhaps it was just one of those things, a casual pick-up. Okay, so she screwed somebody else occasionally. He couldn't blame her.

Mead sipped the coffee abstractedly. There was no

175

sugar in it but he dispensed with the distraction of asking for some.

No, he could not accept she was just an easy lay! She hated the smart-arses who came to the club and thought they could get into her pants for the price of a bottle of champagne. And she was really excited about the new life they were planning together. She talked all the time about their trip overseas. They had spent hours over maps and brochures working out where they would go and what they would see. Collins must have followed her home. Perhaps he was looking for a way to keep Mead in line. Maybe he had even heard that he was planning to quit. Karen might have let it slip to someone. She would never let Collins spoil their plans, but she would have to keep him sweet.

Where the hell could she have gone? He had to find her quickly to answer the questions that were burning in his throat.

It was just after midday when he decided to check out the Capricorn Club. It was only a few streets away and there was a chance that Karen had gone there to see how badly it was damaged.

Mead found the manager sweeping broken glass from the footpath outside the club. The display case by the arched doorway had been smashed, but a photo of Karen in black dancing tights, sequinned costume and a head spray of ostrich feathers was among those still pinned to the board.

The manager stopped sweeping and leaned on his broom as Mead approached.

'I know this place has got the reputation of being a pretty wild town, but this is ridiculous,' he grinned.

'Think yourself lucky you've still got walls standing,' Mead told him. 'The suburbs have been wiped out. It's unbelievable.'

'Yeah? There's nothing on the radio. I've been trying

to tune in on the trannie but the whole lot's dead. The phone's out too. I wonder how long it will take them to sort out this mess.'

Mead shrugged his shoulders.

'Listen, I'm looking for Karen. She's not at the flat. Has she been over here this morning?'

A sudden look of recognition flashed across the man's face.

'Of course!' he responded. 'I was trying to place you, but there are always so many faces around this place that it's difficult to remember who's who.'

Mead nodded and waited for him to continue.

'Karen? No, Karen hasn't been round this morning. Haven't seen her since she left last night. We packed in the show soon after midnight. It was so noisy they could hardly hear the band. Damn shame really. We had a full house all ready to booze on all night and we had to shut the place down. It was probably just as well. Someone was bound to have been hurt when the windows started blowing in.'

'Did she leave on her own?'

'No. I'm pretty sure she went off with this bloke she knew. He was here all evening. He's one of our regulars.'

'A big fair-haired bloke, smartly dressed with a green ring on his left hand?'

'That's him. What's his name? I should know it. The wife will remember.'

He strolled to the door of the club and called inside.

'Glenda! Glenda!'

Mead heard a woman's voice respond

'What's the name of that bloke who was with Karen last night? You know, the tall guy who drinks bourbon.'

He re-emerged from the doorway.

'That's it—Pete,' he told Mead triumphantly. 'Pete

somebody or other. Don't know the surname, but he comes from Sydney. Turns up here every couple of weeks on business and always drops into the club.'

A bulldozer was pushing the wreckage to the sides of the street as Mead walked back to the flat. The sudden roar of the engine and the grating scrape of metal jarred on his already taut nerves. There were crowds on the streets now, stepping carefully through the debris and staring in astonishment at the ruins of a city. Many were helping themselves to food and clothing from the shattered shops, taking away all they could carry. Two young men came hurrying out of a bottle store with their arms laden with bottles of wine. Almost as soon as they were out of the place one bottle was dropped, spreading red wine in a glistening pool on the roadway. A shopkeeper was putting the finishing touches to a warning he had painted in red on the boards he had nailed across his doorway: 'Looters will be shot!!'

Karen and Collins! He couldn't explain it away now. They knew each other well. They met regularly. In fact it appeared they met each time Collins was in Darwin to collect the drugs.

Mead felt quite sick. The thought that she had been with the Sydney hood on the nights before she had welcomed Mead so warmly to her bed turned his stomach. The jealousy was bad enough, but there was fear in Mead too, a growing fear that he had been fooled, played for a sucker, that his plans and dreams had collapsed like the houses of Darwin.

Karen had not returned to the flat. Mead stood in her bedroom looking around at the jumbled array of feminine accessories and wondering if there was anything there anywhere to give him a clue about her relationship with Collins. He started rummaging through the drawers. Underwear, nylons, handkerchiefs. In a dressing-table drawer, scattered amongst a variety of necklaces and earrings, were some letters with Sydney postmarks. He picked one up and looked at the sender's name on the back. Apparently from one of her girlfriends. He took the letter from the envelope and read it. He got more irritable, angry with Karen, as he searched on without finding anything to give him a clue to the nature of her deception.

He didn't know what was there to find, except that it was something to justify the anger he already felt. When he confronted her, when he accused her of betraying his faith and their future, he needed something more solid than shadowy suspicion to thrust in her face.

As his groping, trembling hands failed to provide him with proof, he searched on with masochistic fervour. He must prove her treachery. He wanted her to have lied to him, to have acted the whore. It would make it all so simple.

He took the handbags one by one from the shelf in the wardrobe, tipping them up over the bed to examine any contents. Most of them were empty and there was nothing of significance in the rest. A lipstick, a few coins, an old raffle ticket.

He was about to close the wardrobe door when he noticed the suitcase half buried on the floor beneath a dozen pairs of shoes. There was something familiar about that suitcase. He bent down and pulled it out of the wardrobe, spilling some of the shoes on to the bedroom lino. He put the case on to the bed and reached for the catches. It was locked. He tried to remember in which drawer he had seen the keys. He was tense with anticipation. He knew where he had seen the case before, at least not this one but an identical design. He had seen it every fortnight in the Buffalo motel when Collins had taken the drugs from Mead's attaché-cases and stacked them in the compartment concealed under its false bottom. The only difference between that case and this was that Collins's was grey and Karen's blue.

The second key he tried unlocked it. Some of Karen's clothing had been thrown carelessly inside. Mead put it out on the bed and inserted a nail file between the side and the bottom of the case. The bottom lifted out easily revealing the shallow compartment beneath. A paper bag was in one corner. Inside was one of the brown sealed envelopes of heroin he had seen Collins putting so often into the bottom of his own case, and a batch of small plastic containers used for selling street deals to the addicts.

Mead put the suitcase back in order in the bottom of the wardrobe and lay down on the damp bed, his hands clasped behind his head, staring at the ceiling.

There was nothing to do now but to wait for Karen.

Chapter Fifteen

The nauseous, pervading odour of the dead filled the passageway of the police station as Mike Lindsay headed for the Commissioner's 5 p.m. briefing. A large room on the upstairs floor was being used as an emergency mortuary and the corpses were obviously already decomposing in the hot, wet air. Lindsay paused to peer through the open doorway as he passed. There were about forty bodies, uncovered and laid out in neat rows on the floor surrounded by a spreading pinkish stain of blood as wounds were washed by the afternoon rain dripping from the ceiling. He stared sadly for a moment at the mutilated, broken remains of the children and found himself wondering if before night came they had managed to sneak a look at the Christmas presents they would not live to receive. Did it matter anyway? A sound in the corridor behind him made him turn. Another corpse was being brought in.

There was a buzz of conversation coming from a large room beyond the operations centre. Lindsay shouldered his way in through the crowd of police officers standing waiting for the Commissioner to address them. Few were wearing any semblance of a uniform. They had obviously grabbed any clothing they could lay their hands on. Some wore nothing more than a pair of shorts. The room smelt of sweat, and the heat had already built up to an almost suffocating level.

'Mike!' Lindsay heard the call from somewhere behind him. He turned to see Frank Adams waving at him, his grinning face bobbing up above the shoulders of the taller men in front of him. Lindsay eased his way through to him and grasped Adam's extended hand.

'Thank God you're all right, you old rascal!' Adams declared cheerfully. 'I was beginning to wonder what had happened to you.'

He indicated the bandage high up on Lindsay's left arm which was just visible under the shirt sleeve.

'What have you done there?'

'A bit of a gash,' Lindsay told him. 'I had to go up to the hospital to get it stitched. That's why I haven't been around all day. There were queues lined up for treatment.'

'And someone blasted you with a shotgun too, did they?'

Lindsay grinned and ran his fingers over the lacerated side of his face.

'They had to dig out a bit of glass,' he explained. 'How did you make out?'

'The house has gone. Just nothing left, but we are all okay. We got down into the laundry early and sat it out down there. Luckily it held up somehow. I've just taken the wife and kids over to my parents' place. The old man's got a couple of decent-size tents he's putting up in the garden.'

'Let's hope it doesn't blow up again tonight.'

Adams nodded. 'If it does we're all finished,' he said.

There was a hush in the conversation at the front of the room.

'Could you find a chair from somewhere I could stand on?' The voice was cultured and distinctive. Two officers hurried out to fetch a chair.

From the back of the room Lindsay saw the Commissioner's head and shoulders appear above the crowd. His grey hair had obviously not seen a comb that day and he was not in uniform. Lindsay could see the green and white of a casual shirt.

'That's better,' said the Commissioner, looking across the ragged ranks of his men.

'I'm sorry you have nothing to sit on. The chairs have all gone to the refugee centres. It's as hot as hell in here and I won't keep you long but I felt it important to call you together to tell you as much as I know and to outline our immediate objectives.

'First of all, gentlemen . . .' He looked around hesitantly, adding with an apologetic nod 'and ladies . . . I want to thank you all for being here. I know many of you have suffered great personal tragedies and we can all see those who are injured. It is a great tribute to your devotion to duty that you are here at all. We have something like a ninety-per-cent turn-out of personnel. For all we know the others may be dead or seriously injured. We have no clear picture yet of the extent of this disaster.

'I have just come from a meeting of our emergency services committee and I can tell you this—we have already recovered more than forty dead, at least a hundred seriously injured have been admitted to what is left of the hospital, many of them requiring major surgery, and well over five hundred minor casualties have been treated as outpatients.

'An initial aerial survey had estimated that ninety per cent of all houses are either completely destroyed or rendered uninhabitable. There is no power, no water supply, no sewerage and both radio stations and the television channel have been knocked out. So we have a population of some forty-five thousand sitting out there in the rain, most of them homeless, with no essential services and no way of communicating with them.'

There was a murmur of muffled comment in the room which faded quickly as the Commissioner continued.

'We have two cars with P.A. systems on the road and more are being fitted out but our main means of communication with the population for a start at least is going to be word of mouth. I want every one of you to talk and keep talking to people as you go about your tasks and to tell those people to pass the information you get here on to their neighbours.

'The first thing to tell them is that help is on the way. Furthermore we have just received a message that the fleet has been ordered to put to sea laden to the gunwales with relief supplies and equipment. Of course, it will take them at least five days to get here from Sydney but it's a comfort to know they are on their way.

'The Natural Disasters Organisation in Canberra has been alerted to our situation and a relief team is already mobilised. The aircraft is expected here this evening and it will have on board a fully-equipped surgical team and urgent medical supplies. There has also been a prompt response to our request for an airlift of essential supplies such as food, clothing, blankets, tarpaulins, tents and so on. This afternoon we received a signal from Canberra stating that the defence forces are mounting a major relief operation. The R.A.A.F. is combining with the Army to fly in field cooking equipment and rations to feed twenty thousand people for ten days. We are getting ten thousand blankets, five thousand stretchers, twenty large refrigerators, five thousand sets of sheets and pillows and a radio communications package to provide an immediate link with Canberra.

'Regarding communications, all phones are out, of course, and we are reliant entirely on a field radio the Army has put in to give us contact with the defence forces, and our own car radios. Unfortunately these have been limited by damage to our main V.H.F. antenna and we are having to use the cars in relay. However, we have established direct radio links with the hospital and the ambulance station. The P.M.G. boys are working flat out to give us at least one trunk line out of Darwin tonight and set up a link between emergency services.

'As regards external communications, it appears we were for a few hours at least entirely cut off from the rest of Australia. Everything was out, including the Armed Services' radio networks.'

Lindsay gave Adams a nudge.

'God! I bet Canberra was going berserk!' he whispered. 'For all they knew, the place might have been invaded!'

'Luckily a ship came into harbour just before 10 a.m. today and managed to establish a somewhat tenuous morse link with the Marine Operations Centre in Canberra,' the Commissioner continued. 'The ship was our only means of communication at first, but the P.M.G. has now opened a line on the microwave, which we can use from the telephone exchange, and the Armed Services have re-established some kind of communication links, although I understand they are intermittent.

'Now the second thing I want you to tell the people is that we are going to have to evacuate this city. To what extent is undecided at the moment, but I think we might be talking about lifting out twenty thousand or thirty thousand people in a very short space of time. They cannot stay here because there is no longer a city here to support them. Feeding them is going to be a major problem and we will be setting up distribution centres for food and water. Many people have already moved into the schools and turned them into virtual refugee centres, so it is quite likely that these will be used for food distribution along with any other large buildings which are still sufficiently undamaged to afford shelter.

'In a situation such as this there is a serious risk of

disease. People should be encouraged not to use lavatories unless they have sufficient water to flush them, but to dig proper latrines away from their living areas and to attend closely to personal hygiene. Containers of disinfectant will be distributed tomorrow and this should be used where people have no soap and water. Large quantities of typhoid vaccine and tetanus anti-toxin will be flown in over the next few days and a programme of inoculation for the entire community will be implemented.'

The Commissioner took out a handkerchief and mopped the sweat that was running down his face.

'Our major role at this stage is to assist with the injured and the recovery of bodies. It could be days before we can be sure we have got everybody out.

'Our second major task involves the protection of property. There is already some looting going on and we can expect this to become more widespread in the coming days. Quite frankly, with no food distribution yet organised, I am not concerned at the moment about families helping themselves to food which is going to rot anyway, but we are going to have to clamp down hard on trespassing and theft of personal property and goods from shops and warehouses. Inspector Simmonds is working now on a roster of anti-looting patrols which will extend throughout the city and suburbs as roads are progressively cleared. All cars, including those not involved in the anti-looting patrols, will be equipped with firearms. We want to keep a low profile on this. We don't want police walking around brandishing guns but we have a situation here with the potential for a complete breakdown in law and order and we have to be ready for it should it occur. As far as the public is concerned, you are carrying guns to shoot stray dogs. Any dog seen wandering the streets on its own is to be shot on sight. We don't want a situation developing where we have starving animals hunting in packs and spreading disease.'

The Commissioner paused and glanced at a piece of paper he had taken from a pocket.

'Well, I think that's about all for the moment, gentlemen and ladies. It is a necessarily brief outline but I don't want to keep you here a moment longer than I have to. If there are any urgent questions I will do my best to answer them but I think we should be getting about our business as quickly as possible.'

He looked around the room, and a hand went up in one of the front lines.

'Could you just tell us, Commissioner, when the evacuation will start?' a young officer asked.

'The answer to that is as soon as we can get aircraft in here. The airport is in a hell of a mess at the moment and there is some feverish work going on down there to clear the main runway in time for the arrival of the first relief plane, which is already on its way. The reports we have say that there are light aircraft piled up on one another and upside down all over the tarmac; in fact I hear that a D.C.3 was blown over a hangar and dumped on top of a R.A.A.F. house.'

'Dropped in for Christmas,' Lindsay whispered to Adams.

'The new terminal building has been virtually destroyed,' the Commissioner continued. 'All navigational instruments, radar and landing aids are out of action. If this plane gets in tonight it will have to land on a pretty rudimentary flare-path and we may be called on to make some of our cars available to help light it. Every aircraft that comes in with supplies will be back-loaded with refugees, the first priority going to the seriously injured.'

The Commissioner pointed to another officer who was indicating he had a question to ask.

'What is the situation with people taken into custody, Commissioner? Can we handle them? I understand that the cells here are already full.'

The Commissioner nodded.

'Yes, we have a critical situation there at the moment. There was considerable damage last night to the gaol of Fannie Bay. The remand huts were demolished and even some stone walls of the old prison building collapsed. A few prisoners were injured, about a dozen are unaccounted for. We don't know if they are dead, trapped in the wreckage or have just taken off. We had eighty-four in custody, including six females, and there was no way we could keep them at the gaol so we transferred them to the police cells here where at least we have got our own power being generated. Now, what is happening is that prisoners on short sentences, say up to fourteen days or something like that, are being released. I think all the females will go, and I think it quite likely that later we will obtain permission to release prisoners who are serving longer sentences. It depends what happens. But the answer to your question is yes, we do have a problem, we certainly don't want to take anyone else into custody if we can possibly avoid it, but of course there will undoubtedly be arrests that have to be made.'

Lindsay raised his hand as soon as the Commissioner stopped speaking.

'Mike Lindsay, sir. Federal Narcotics. I have a prisoner in custody whose assistance is required in connection with a matter still under investigation. I would like to request his retention. Could you please tell me who I should make that request to? My second question is would it be possible for me to get an urgent message through to Canberra?'

The Commissioner shook his head with a smile.

'Mr Lindsay, I appreciate your predicament and your

188

enthusiasm to pursue your investigations but obviously the preservation of life, the evacuation of the injured and the need for essential emergency supplies must take priority and we can offer you no special consideration. I suggest you go across the road to the court office where the matter of the release of prisoners is being handled and, as for contacting Canberra, I think your best bet is to try the telephone exchange where you may be able to persuade them to give you a minute on the line if it ever gets clear. I'm afraid, Mr Lindsay, that in this situation you are just a refugee like the rest of us and probably with fewer problems than most.'

The Commissioner stepped down from his chair and the meeting broke up with a buzz of conversation as the police filed from the room.

Torrential rain was peppering the pools along the gutters as Lindsay and Adams sprinted across the road to the Supreme Court building. They mounted the steps two at a time and burst through the doors to stand panting in the corridor, shaking and brushing the water from themselves. The place was packed with people, some half naked, others in night-clothes or wrapped in blankets. A few were stretched out full-length on the floor and others were sitting with their backs against the walls. Children ran up and down the passageway making it echo with their din. Many of the adults wore bloodstained bandages or carried the scars of Tracy with the blood congealed on their faces. Most of them sat in silence, staring ahead, taking no notice of what was happening around them.

Adams indicated the corridor to the right.

'This way.'

They walked past the outstretched legs of the refugees.

'These people are in a state of shock, Frank,' said Lindsay.

189

'At least they are out of the rain,' Adams replied.

The court clerk's office was in a state of total confusion. He was on his hands and knees picking up documents and correspondence from the floor when they walked into the room. Filing-cabinet drawers were hanging open, and torn and screwed up files and papers were strewn all over the office. He got to his feet and threw the batch he had in his hand on the desk as Adams greeted him.

'What a mess!' he exclaimed, waving a hand at the office in general. 'The damn hippies got in here, bust open the files and generally turned the place inside out.'

'Yeah, I can see what you mean,' said Adams. He indicated Lindsay. 'This is Mike Lindsay, Federal Narcotics, John. Look, we're sorry to worry you, but have you got a list of the blokes brought down from Fannie Bay? It's important.'

The clerk rubbed a hand across his eyes.

'I've got the names here somewhere of those that are in the police cells.' He started pushing the papers on his desk aside. 'The warden's office is supposed to be letting us have a full list of prisoners but I've no idea when that is likely to arrive.

'Ah, yes. Here we are.' He picked up a batch of foolscap sheets which had been clipped together and handed it to Adams.

'The asterisks are the ones that have been released.'

Adams ran his finger down the names while Lindsay checked them with him.

'No Mead,' said Adams.

'No Mead,' Lindsay repeated in a tone that suggested he had already resigned himself to expect the name to be missing. He turned to the clerk.

'Are you confident that this is a complete list of those still in custody?'

'It should be. The police did a roll call of the cells this

morning. If your bloke was in Fannie Bay last night and his name's not there it means that he is either dead, injured or free as a bird.'

Lindsay nodded. 'He would have been in the remand huts,' he said.

'Yes, well they got wiped out. Part of the fence was flattened and a few of them ran for it. Can't say I blame them. It was a matter of finding somewhere to stay alive.'

The clerk accepted the list back from Adams and resumed his crawl around the office floor.

'If it's any consolation,' he told Lindsay, 'your man being only on remand, he would have been released by now anyway. We can't hold them forever in custody without the sanction of the court and heaven knows how long it will be before that sits again.'

He called after them as they were about to walk out of the door.

'Frank, take a look in Supreme Court One on your way out. That ought to interest you as a Drug Squad man. The hippies have taken the place over and I bet it'll be the first time you've seen pot being smoked in court.'

The strong, distinctive smell of burning marijuana wafted out of the courtroom door as Lindsay and Adams opened it. There were about thirty youngsters spread around the court, lying on the floor or lounging in the jury-box and at the counsels' table. Empty beer cans had obviously been thrown at the bench where a heavily-built, bearded youth was seated in the senior judge's chair wearing a judicial wig and red robe. He was dragging deeply on a joint. He caught sight of the two men peering in the back of the court and beckoned in their direction as he exhaled a thin cloud of smoke.

'Bring the prisoners forward,' he called.

An attractive girl with long dark hair sitting next to

him started giggling and clambered up to stand on the bench, almost falling as she got tangled up in the long judge's robe she was wearing. She danced along the bench, then stopped to turn and stare imperiously at Adams, who had taken a few steps into the courtroom. She raised her arm to point at him, pulling open the robe with her other hand to reveal she was completely naked under it.

'I sentence you to six months' hard pot-smoking,' she said in as deep a voice as she could manage. The statement was greeted with general hilarity.

Adams turned to Lindsay with a grin.

'Ah well, the happy people are having fun anyway,' he remarked. 'Let's get out of here before I start believing my eyes.'

The youth in the judge's chair yelled out before they reached the door.

'It's all legal now, Adams! Your precious laws don't mean a thing!'

It had stopped raining but water was still pouring from a section of broken guttering on the Supreme Court building and slapping noisily on to the concrete behind them as the two men hesitated at the top of the front steps. The wet air enclosed them like a warm blanket.

The last contemptuous call of the pot-smoking young man in the judge's wig was still echoing in Lindsay's mind. Your precious laws don't mean a thing!

'You know, he's right, Frank,' he said to Adams. 'If Mead is fool enough to go to Burrows and tell him he has been arrested, he's a dead man.'

'Just another cyclone victim found amongst the rubble?'

Lindsay nodded grimly.

'Mead is dispensable. The pipeline's finished. Once Burrows knows that, he'll tidy up the loose ends, make sure there is nothing left that can lead us to the syndicate. That's his job.'

They walked down the steps in silence. At the bottom Lindsay took Adams by the arm.

'Frank, I know you've got your own problems, but could you do me one more favour? Would you run a check over the morgue to see if either of them has turned up?'

'Sure. That's no worry. And what are you going to be up to?'

Lindsay looked away from him when he replied.

'I'm going to find Burrows. We've got enough to hold him on suspicion of trafficking and importation, and if I can only get a message through to Canberra we may be in time to get the Indonesians to pick up the plane in Bali with the consignment still on board.'

'Hoping for an extradition order on the pilot?'

'It's the only way we are going to get him now, for he won't be flying in here again for a while until they can set up a new connection at this end. He's Australian and we've got a pretty good working arrangement with the Indonesians.'

'How can you be sure he is still in Bali? He might have already made the first hop and be waiting at Kupang.'

Lindsay shook his head.

'Burrows phoned through yesterday afternoon and told him to wait until he gave him the all clear. They've probably got something like three kilos of high-grade heroin on the plane which would fetch close on a million dollars in Sydney. I guess Burrows reckoned it was safer keeping it waiting in the Balinese jungle than sitting at an official airport like Kupang.'

'And where do you reckon you're going to find him?'

'I'll check the hospital again first and if he's not there I'll just have to sit it out at the motel. He didn't come back there last night but all his gear was still in his room this morning. One thing is certain – he's had no more chance of getting out of this town today than the rest of us. We are all stuck here together.'

The bulldozers had cleared pathways through the wreckage in the main city streets by the time darkness brought an uncanny stillness to Darwin.

Lindsay walked alone in the blackness, keeping to the centre of the road. Occasionally a car passed by, dazzling him momentarily with the glare of its headlights and lighting up the confusion of debris around him. He was surprised how much he could see in the moonless night as he moved between the dark silhouettes of broken buildings and leaning light-poles. He might have been walking through a battlefield, a deserted city that had just been bombarded.

It was like a wartime scene at the hospital too. The bustling activity he had witnessed earlier in the day was still going on, with weary medical staff wheeling the injured on trolleys between wards and operating theatres along shadowy corridors illuminated at intervals by pools of yellow light from the emergency lighting. Dishevelled, blood-stained survivors were sitting or stretched out on the floor and benches in the darkened out-patient area where women wearing Red Cross armbands had set up a small mobile canteen and were handing out cardboard cups of coffee and soup.

Lindsay wandered through the crowded wards unchallenged, systematically studying every face. He gazed with growing horror on the rows of mutilated, bandaged victims lying in beds covered with hurriedly-constructed tents of plastic sheeting to protect them from the water dripping from the ceilings. In places large tarpaulins were suspended beneath gaping holes in the roof.

Many of the injured lay staring blankly up into space,

not noticing Lindsay as he leaned over them. Others turned away from him, moaning with pain as they moved. One woman with silent tears running down her cheeks started whimpering as he peered at the man in the next bed. She reached out and caught Lindsay's wrist as he was about to move away.

'Is Frank all right?' she whispered. He gently loosened her grip and placed her hand back by her side.

'Don't worry now,' he told her. 'Try to get some sleep.'

It was after 10 p.m. when he left the hospital and ambulances were still bringing in casualties who were being hurried along the covered walkway between the wards on stretchers and in wheelchairs.

He could not be sure that Burrows was not somewhere in the hospital, but it seemed more likely now that he was not among the seriously injured.

After the activity of the hospital, the stillness and silence of the dark streets as he walked back to the city centre was uncanny.

An old man bumped into him in the dark and took hold of his arm. At first Lindsay thought he was a drunk, but he soon concluded he was genuinely lost and bewildered.

'I'm looking for my sister's place,' he said. 'I'm calling in on her for Christmas, for a surprise, you know.'

He looked around, still clasping Lindsay's arm.

'What's happened here? I can't find anything I recognise.'

'Where have you come from?' Lindsay asked.

'Just come up the track. I've been walking for hours. It's all so dark.'

Lindsay started to lead him down the street, but the old man resisted.

'No, I'll find it. It must be around here somewhere.'

'You'd better come with me to the police station. That's your best bet.'

The old man was reluctant.

'There's a big house on the corner of the street,' he said firmly. 'I'll know it when I see it. It was somewhere along here.'

Gently, Lindsay guided him along the road.

'What's going on?' he asked. 'I can't understand it.'

Lindsay knew people were all round them, but he could see little of them. A few had lit fires to cook on and give themselves some light. Some had managed to find oil lamps or candles. He could see them sitting quietly in little shelters they had built for themselves in the ruins of their homes with the soft glow of the flickering light reflected on their faces. But most of them were without even a candle, absorbed by the darkness so that it came as a surprise for him suddenly to hear the cry of a child or some muffled conversation from the gaping wreck of a house and to realise that somewhere in the tangled mess a family was settling down for the night.

He left the old man still protesting at the police station and by the time he got back to the motel he was exhausted. His injured arm was throbbing with pain. He had got little sleep the night before, cramped together with the other guests on the floor of the dining-room where they were safe from the flying glass.

The foyer was lit by flickering lanterns and candles. The carpet had been ripped out to leave a bare concrete floor and most of the suspended ceiling sections had gone, exposing a maze of silver air-conditioning ducts and pipes above the hanging framework.

The night manager, dressed in shorts and T-shirt instead of his usual uniform, greeted Lindsay as he walked up to the reception desk.

'There's no point in giving you a key,' he grinned. 'There's hardly a door left on its hinges.'

He handed him a candle and a box of matches.

'If your bed is dry you'll probably find someone has already grabbed it. You'll have to find yourself a room, if you can.'

There was a note from Frank Adams in Lindsay's pigeon-hole. He had checked the morgues without finding Burrows.

'With a bit of luck we'll be serving packets of cornflakes from seven o'clock,' said the receptionist.

By the light of his candle Lindsay climbed the bare emergency staircase to the sixth floor. The scene in the corridors reminded him of the hospital with bedraggled men, women and children moaning and moving restlessly as they tried to get some sleep on the hard floor. The candle blew out several times as he passed open doorways, plunging the corridor into total blackness until his fumbling hands struck a light that softly illuminated once again the huddled, hunched figures of the refugees.

Three people were asleep on Burrows's bed. His clothes were still in the room and, in the wardrobe, was the suitcase which Lindsay had checked earlier in the day. The locks had given him no trouble. A return air ticket to Sydney, and, tucked away under the false bottom, an envelope containing five thousand dollars in fifty-dollar notes, presumably Mead's payment for delivering the drugs.

Satisfied Burrows would return to the room before leaving Darwin, Lindsay found himself a vacant space amongst the recumbent forms in the corridor and settled down to get some sleep. At least he had managed to get a message through to Canberra which should sew up the Bali end.

The air was already becoming foul with the smell of

sweaty, unwashed bodies and the unhealthy stench from the inoperative lavatories.

Lindsay lay awake for a long while in the darkness, listening to the constant crying of the children and the occasional adult voice muttering, sometimes screaming out, as the survivors relived in their sleep the terror of the night before.

Tomorrow perhaps the main highway would have been cleared enough for him to drive out to the airstrip and tell Jamieson that he was wasting his time sitting out there with his bird circus waiting for a plane that would never arrive. He smiled at the thought of the officious inspector in his smart Fauna Squad uniform rationing out the bird seed and waiting for an instruction from Canberra telling him what to do next.

He tried to conjure up the scene in his imagination but the other images were too strong. Behind his closed eyes he could still see rows of roofless houses and shambling refugees. Slowly he slipped into a fitful sleep.

Chapter Sixteen

Very carefully the girl with the long, brown legs poured some water from a plastic bucket into the cup Mead was holding.

'That's all you get for cleaning your teeth,' she told him.

She seemed to have taken charge of the place, cooking the meals, organising the rations for the crowd that had requisitioned Karen's flat. It was impossible to say how many were camping there. Judging from the array of camp beds, mattresses and cushions spread across the floor under the remaining section of roof, Mead reckoned there must be about twenty, but there was too much coming and going to be sure. The doors had been blown off their hinges and people walked in off the street during the night, stepping gingerly in the blackness over the sleeping figures to find a space wide enough for them to lie down on the bare floor.

Like the rest of them, the girl was young. Probably in her early twenties. Mead liked the look of her. As he freshened up his mouth with a toothbrush and tube of toothpaste he had found in the bathroom, he watched her moving between the kitchen and the patio where half a dozen people were sitting around the large table now covered with dirty plates, cups and empty beer cans. She was wearing an old pair of sandals and ragged, faded shorts that were tight under her crotch but in the general disorder she was parading about like a hostess at a dinner party.

Mead rinsed his mouth with the last of the water and spat it out on to the remains of a flower bed. Her toffy

English accent irritated him. He would have enjoyed taking her down a peg or two. He amused himself as his eyes followed her by imagining how she would squeal if he grabbed hold of that long black hair and had a feel of those brown breasts of hers.

She knew the way he was watching her.

'Hasn't your girlfriend turned up yet?' she asked him as he sat down at the table and ripped the top off a can of warm beer.

Mead shook his head. 'She'll be back,' he assured her.

'We're going to have to find some water today,' she announced to those sitting round the table. 'We didn't catch much from the rain last night.'

'What do we want water for?' a ginger-haired youth wanted to know. 'We got enough booze from that pub last night to last us a month.' He indicated a pile of cardboard cartons of canned beer which had been stacked against the wall.

'We've got to clean up these dishes and, believe it or not, I wouldn't mind having a wash sometime,' the hostess explained patiently.

'We'd better organise some search parties,' suggested the man Mead had seen digging the garden latrine the previous day. 'How many of us have still got a usable car?'

Two of the men raised their hands.

'I'm very low on petrol,' one said.

'There's plenty of wrecks around to syphon some from,' the other told him. 'A mate of mine's got a caravan parked out at Casuarina. If we could get over there we might be able to get hold of the cooker and some bottled gas. He wouldn't mind us borrowing it. He's gone down to Sydney for Christmas.

'You'd better watch out you don't get yourself shot,' his girlfriend warned.

'Yeah, the cops are walking around with rifles and

belts of ammunition,' the ginger-headed youth added excitedly. 'One of them told me they would shout only one challenge to anyone they saw nosing around and then they'd shoot.'

'Well, we've got to find food and water,' insisted the hostess.

'And a change of underpants,' someone added with a laugh. 'In this sort of situation what is looting and what is simply surviving?'

The discussion was interrupted by the arrival of a couple carrying bottles of champagne in their arms.

'Got them from the wine bar,' the man explained. 'The place is wrecked and everyone is helping themselves.'

'That's absolutely marvellous!' the hostess exclaimed derisively. 'All I want is a shower and all you've got is champagne!' She raised a hand to her head in mock despair.

'Well, you're not washing in this,' he replied, uncorking the first bottle. 'They didn't send it all the way from France to hose down sweaty armpits.'

His wife laughed.

'Don't talk to him about showers. He had a brainwave this morning and spent an hour sawing off our down-pipe and hanging a tank under the gutter so that we could use the tap as a shower. When he got it finished he realised we didn't have any roof on to catch the rain!'

The deep throb of aircraft engines filled the sky and they looked up to see an R.A.A.F. Hercules flying low across the city.

'Looks as though the cavalry's arriving,' the latrine digger remarked.

When the others left on their scavenging expeditions, Mead went back to Karen's bedroom and lay down on the bed. He had been dozing for about an hour when she walked in the door. Her exclamation of surprise woke him.

'Ray! What on earth are you doing here?'

He stared blankly at her for a moment, taken off guard, as he often was, by her sensual attractiveness, his immediate feelings a mixture of anger and desire. He swung his feet to the floor as she moved towards him.

'Darling, how did you manage to get into town? I thought you would still be stuck out at the airstrip.'

He took her by the shoulders as she went to kiss him.

'Where the hell have you been?' he snapped angrily holding her away from him.

She hesitated for a moment, glancing up at him anxiously. 'I've been over at a girlfriend's place. Don't be silly, darling. Kiss me. I'm so glad to see you.'

She moved through his resistance, drawing his mouth down to hers, immediately absorbing him in the fascination of her familiarity. The moist softness of her full lips, the taste, the smell of her, were unlike any other. He could never recall her entirely while he was away, but each time he returned to her arms he remembered. It always surprised him that he had access to her, that someone he desired so much gave herself to him so easily. She could arouse him instantly, effortlessly. Then, having begun where others finished, she would deliberately fan the flames of his lust, whispering his own obscenities into his ear, destroying all control, unafraid of the power which she would drain from him almost carelessly, finally dominating him by her total submission.

Her eager mouth grew more insistent and her warm body moved against his as his passion for her overwhelmed all other emotions. She broke off the embrace and fell back on to the bed, stretching herself provocatively, mocking him with her eyes.

'Well, come on,' she sighed. 'We can talk later.'

He glanced towards the door.

'Someone may come in.'

'Then you'd better hurry. Possession, they say, is nine-tenths of the law.'

He reached down and ripped open her blouse. She laughed and wriggled out of her panties as he took hold of them.

'Now, tell me all about the little hitch-hiker you picked up this trip,' she breathed as he lowered himself on to her. 'Or didn't you manage to find one to practise on?'

Mead's need for her passed quickly. As they lay back on the bed he stared up at the gaping ceiling, trying to sort out his thoughts and emotions and work out a place for him to begin to discuss them with her without catapulting them straight into a flaming row.

But it was Karen who first resumed the conversation.

'So when did you get into town?'

'Early on Christmas Eve.'

'You mean that you were here for the cyclone? Where were you when it hit?'

Mead turned to look at her.

'In Fannie Bay gaol.'

She sat up on the bed, propping herself with one hand as she stared down at him, anxiously searching his face to see if he was joking. She could see that he wasn't.

'What happened? Tell me the whole story.'

He reached over the side of the bed to pick up his shirt from the floor and take a packet of cigarettes from the pocket. Karen shook her head when he offered her one.

'Old Habib and I got jumped at Powell Creek. The cops were waiting there for me when I drove up to collect the birds. There was a wildlife guy hiding in the back of the old man's van, a plainclothes bloke and a couple more in a police Land Cruiser. One of them stayed behind to drive back the truck while me and Habib were brought up to Fannie Bay.'

'My God! Do you think they know anything about the drugs?'

'Of course they know about the drugs! What do you think they wanted the truck for? They were going to take it to the strip to meet the plane. They knew the whole lot.'

'How could they? They must have been guessing. There was nothing to connect you with the stuff. You didn't have any of it on you, did you?'

'No, of course I didn't, but I tell you they had everything sewn up. This Lindsay bloke was telling me as we were driving up to Darwin. He knew where the airstrip was, what time the plane was due and where I made the delivery. He was trying to get me to make a full statement. He told me they had had the whole operation under observation for some time.'

Karen scrambled out of bed and started to put on her clothes.

'You didn't admit anything did you?'

'I stayed right clammed up. I don't think they've got enough evidence on me to pin me with the drug rap.'

He was out of bed too now and stepping into his shorts as Karen fumbled through the hangers in the wardrobe searching for a clean blouse.

'And where do you think you're going?' he asked her. 'Going to tip off your boyfriend?'

He stubbed out the cigarette, less than half smoked.

'What are you talking about?' she replied without looking round.

'I know all about you and Collins. I know he was with you on Christmas Eve.'

'Well, what does that mean?' she continued. 'Look, I met the guy at the club, he offered to drive me home and I asked him in for a coffee. That's all there was to it.'

'You asked him in for a screw, you mean. He stayed the night.'

'The whole town was blowing down,' she shouted angrily. 'There was no way he could leave.'

He moved towards her threateningly.

'You lying whore! You've known Collins as long as you've known me. I know you meet him every time he comes here.'

He grabbed her wrist, bending her arm back angrily.

'Now, tell me. What the hell is going on?'

'Let go of me, you creep.' She struggled to free herself. 'You don't own me. I've got a right to have my own friends.'

'Friends! That guy's a hardened crim, a stand-over man. He's not just a courier, you know. He's up to his ears in the Sydney drug racket.'

'And what do you think you are? At least he's not dumb enough to get caught . . .'

Mead swung his right fist and caught her on the side of the head. The force of the blow flung her across the bed, where she lay clasping both hands to her face, still and silent as though she feared the slightest movement would provoke him to hit her again.

Taken suddenly by a wave of remorse, he leaned over her and stroked the back of her head. He had not meant it to be like this.

'I'm sorry, baby. I'm really sorry. You shouldn't speak to me like that.'

He sat on the bed beside her.

'We've got to get away now. We'll have to cut short our plans and leave the country. Just like we planned to, but we've got to do it straight away. I can get someone to run the truck for me. It will give us an income.'

She turned on him savagely. There were tears in her eyes but she was not crying.

'I'm not going anywhere with you,' she yelled.

'You're finished. Now get out of here and leave me alone.'

She got up, still holding the side of her face, and took the suitcase from the bottom of the wardrobe. Mead watched her in silence as she opened the lid and started piling clothes into it.

'What are you doing? Don't be crazy, baby. You can't walk out just like that. What about all our plans? What about the trip? Don't you want to go overseas any more?'

'Look, I told you. We're finished, Ray.'

'Why? What the hell's so different? I've got enough dough saved to give us a good time. It's just that we won't have as much as we'd planned.'

She was taking no notice of him. The suitcase was almost full and she was searching through the last drawer in the dressing-table. Mead felt sick in his stomach. She seemed so determined. She had hurriedly grabbed a basic selection of clothes and her most important personal possessions and was likely to walk out the door any second.

'It's Collins, isn't it? You're going to him now. You're going to warn him.'

'There's no sense in letting him get arrested.'

'Oh, no, you don't, baby. You're not going anywhere until we've sorted this whole thing out.'

He reached past her and tipped the suitcase off the bed, spilling the contents out over the floor. Picking up the empty case, he scrabbled unsuccessfully to lift the false bottom.

'And what are you doing with this shit in the bottom of your case?' he shouted, looking around desperately for a nail file.

She made a run for the door but he was too quick for her, grabbing her arm and pulling her back into the room.

'Bitch!'

'For Christ's sake, let me go!' she screamed. 'Look, Ray, I've got to tell him they're on to us. He's trying to get a message through to bring the plane in, and if it flies into a trap we're all gone. You'll be in it too. Your truck's at the strip.'

'You've been working with Collins all along!' he gasped, recalling how it had all began, the way she had casually arranged for them to meet at the Capricorn.

'You got your compensation,' she yelled. 'And his name's Burrows, Pete Burrows, not Collins.'

'You never did intend to come away with me! It was all a con, right from the beginning, just to keep me running the stuff.'

'They would never have let me get away. I was too valuable to them here.'

'Peddling the stuff through the club?'

She nodded.

'It started off as a special favour to me when Pete let me have some for a couple of friends. Then Sydney decided to use my contacts to set up a local distribution chain. It had hardly got going and they had hopes of a big market here. I was the key to it, so they weren't going to let me leave.'

'We could have made a run for it. We could have got away. We can get away now.'

'You really are dumb, aren't you?' she snapped angrily. 'Look, Pete and I aren't exactly married but I'm his woman, okay? He brought me up here from Sydney and got the whole operation going. He told me to find a sucker to run the stuff and to keep the guy happy while he was doing the job. You know, that means in bed and everything.'

Mead was staring at her disbelievingly. She was enjoying hurting him. Her face was still stinging.

'That's when you came along,' she said savagely.

207

'You were the sucker, the bunny. Now let's forget the whole thing. It's over. Okay?'

The back of her head banged hard against the wall as his hands tightened round her throat. The sickness in his stomach had been replaced by the blind fury contorting his face as though he too was being strangled as his fingers tore into her neck.

He did not hear Burrows come into the room. The first he knew was a hand on his shoulder spinning him round and an explosive blow in the stomach which blacked out everything before he had a chance to work out what was going on. He was on the floor. Karen's voice was faint as though it was coming from the next room.

'The cops are on to us . . . arrested . . . staked out the strip . . .'

Mead was retching, doubled up clasping his stomach, too weak to attempt to stand.

'Get your things,' Burrows told Karen. 'I'll deal with this bastard.'

Unbuttoning his shirt, he took his 357 magnum from its shoulder holster as he walked across to the bed and picked up a pillow.

'Don't kill him, Pete, please,' Karen pleaded.

'Shut up and get that case packed,' he snapped back. 'We'll dump him in the debris. Could have been a looter.'

Mead was moaning, trying to roll up on to his knees as Burrows bent over him.

'What's going on?' asked a voice from the doorway. It was the latrine digger poking his head round the door.

He looked long at Burrows crouched with the revolver in his hand over the squirming figure on the floor.

'Christ!' he said, and disappeared.

Burrows stood up and put the gun away.

'Come on, let's go! We'll pick up my stuff on the way.'

He took deliberate aim with the toe of his right shoe and savagely kicked Mead once on the side of the knee.

They left the room in a rush. The latrine digger was helping Mead on to his feet almost before he realised they had gone.

'What was that all about?'

'Quick, help me to the door,' Mead gasped.

He put an arm round the man's shoulder and struggled out of the room. His right leg was in agony when he put his full weight on it. They got to the vacant front doorway just in time to see a battered light blue Valiant driving off.

'I'll be okay,' said Mead, letting go of the man. 'I've got to catch them.'

He scrambled through the general debris in the courtyard and got over the fallen palm tree lying across the driveway entrance, sitting on it to swing his legs across. He started limping painfully along the centre of the road, looking anxiously for the shop he had spotted the day before. The front door was still on the pavement under a shattered neon sign that had once advertised the place as a sports store.

Mead glanced up and down the street. There was no one close by. The shop was fairly dark inside, for the ceiling had remained intact despite the fact that the windows had been blown out front and rear. Mead stepped across broken glass and picked his way through fallen display stands and scattered equipment. The blades of the large central ceiling fan had been bent at right angles so that they pointed parallel with one another to the ground. There was a rack full of rifles and shotguns behind the counter. He selected a light-looking .303 repeater, then searched the shelves beneath for the right ammunition. With fumbling fingers he loaded ten shells into the magazine and slipped the rest of the box into his pocket.

Burrows had said they were calling at the motel to get his things. Mead estimated that gave him about ten minutes at the most to get there. The city centre was quiet. People were wandering about aimlessly in the streets in groups of three or four still looking in bewilderment at the damage. On one vacant block about a dozen adults and children were gathered around a sheet of iron set up over a fire on which they were barbecueing meat and sausages. The ragged refugees sitting in the remains of shops and offices on either side of the street took no notice of the figure hobbling past with a rifle in his hand. Those who saw him probably assumed he was a police officer on an anti-looting patrol.

He could see the motel ahead. Karen's car was parked with its back to him by the ornamental fish pond in the driveway. Two men were dipping a yellow plastic garbage bin into the water. As he got closer he saw Karen come running out of the motel carrying a suit-case. The passenger door of the car swung open as she ran up to it. Burrows must have waited in the car while she went in to collect his gear. Mead stopped and raised the rifle to his shoulder. The cross in the telescopic sight moved across the broken rear window of the car. The men with the garbage bin drew it out of the pond and started carrying it between them towards the motel entrance. Mead lowered the rifle as they crossed behind the car, struggling under the weight of the water. He could not get a clear shot.

Desperately he tried to break into a run as the car moved off. It came out of the far entrance of the drive and turned right into the street, heading away from him.

It was accelerating rapidly when he fired. He pumped

three shots into the rear offside tyre and the car slewed to the right, mounted the far kerb and slammed into a low, brick garden wall. Burrows came out of the driver's door in a flash, leapt the wall and ran, crouching low, towards the wreckage of the house.

Karen was standing beside the car as Mead drew level with it.

'You stay put,' he shouted, waving an arm and only half glancing in her direction for fear of losing his focus on the spot where he had last seen Burrows disappearing behind the leaning remains of a steel garage.

Crazy with anger and pain as he was, Mead had more sense than to chase directly after him. Instead he cut across the garden of a smashed stilt house and ducked into the piles of debris which littered the gardens between the two rows of abandoned homes. He squatted down behind a jumbled mass of timber and plasterboard suspended from the edge of the platform floor, sucking in his breath and trying to get his trembling body under control.

From behind his cover he peered at the endless devastation, watching for a movement. All the roofs had gone but many of the ground-level houses still had some walls standing. If there had once been garden fences separating them, they had disappeared so that, with the ground strewn with the universal twisted fragments of buildings and belongings, the area between the rows was a mad maze of desolation.

He could see no sign of Burrows, no hint of movement apart from the odd piece of debris swaying in the gentle breeze. He had to flush him out. He raised the rifle to his shoulder and fired a round in the direction he had last seen him. The bullet sent up a puff of dust as it smacked into the debris.

Damn it, where was the bastard? He might be moving away from him, from house to house.

Mead started working his way between the rows, the rifle held across his chest with his finger tense on the trigger. He stepped awkwardly across sheets of iron and broken beams, groping his way with his foot rather than take his eyes for a second off the confusion of shattered buildings and shadowy forests of round steel floor pillars ahead.

He froze momentarily in reflex reaction when a black cat darted out of the wreckage and raced across the open ground in front of him, hurdling the debris in smooth bounds. Still motionless, he studied the ruins from which it had emerged. Had Burrows disturbed it?

There was the clatter of metal to the right and he swung round instinctively, raising the rifle.

Mead felt the searing pain high on his left arm at the same time that he heard the crack of the revolver. He yelled as the bullet jolted into him but as he hunched up in agony he managed to blast off a one-handed shot in the general direction he had seen Burrows's head pop out from behind a wall.

He could see him scrambling across the wreckage, changing his position. Mead fired another hurried round and heard the bullet ricochet away into the distance with an angry whine. Burrows ducked out of sight, and Mead half stumbled, half fell to the ground behind a refrigerator lying on its side. With a wrecked car at the back of him, he had good cover from both directions and Burrows was now more out in the open than he was. He propped himself against the refrigerator, using its top edge as a rest for the rifle. Burrows bobbed up for a split second and a bullet whirred past Mead's head, punching a hole through the dented roof of the car. Mead didn't move. He still had four shots left in the first magazine and his sight was trained on the spot where Burrows had appeared. He didn't really care if he died now. He could feel the blood flowing down his arm and waves of faintness were washing over him as his consciousness was absorbed by the all-consuming pain. He had to stay conscious long enough to get a clear shot. He had the bloke pinned down. That was all that mattered.

He shook his head and tried to hold concentration. He was peering out now between moments of total blackness. He turned and stretched his face, trying to keep his eyes open but the periods of vision shortened to brief flashes as though he was inside a camera staring out as the shutter clicked. The same unreal picture repeated itself. The barrel of a rifle pointing at a chaotic scene of debris and broken houses. Was this really happening? How long had he been unconscious?

If only he could move, he might be able to fend off the darkness. He pulled the rifle tightly into his shoulder, bringing the telescopic cross to bear once again on the pile of wreckage behind which Burrows was hiding. Suddenly he heard the revolver snap to his right and a bullet slapped against the refrigerator. He swung the rifle round and blasted off another shot. How had Burrows got over there?

His elbow was sticky on the refrigerator, his blood creeping downwards across the door. He adjusted his position to bring the rifle to bear on the area where he had seen Burrows duck down out of the corner of his eye. He could not be sure of the exact spot, but if he could just stay conscious he still had the advantage. Burrows would have to be very lucky to hit him. The pain was roaring in his ears again. A feeling of resignation washed over him just before the darkness.

When the shutter opened again the new picture imprinted itself on his consciousness. He was looking up at the platform of a demolished house right above his protective refrigerator, and Burrows was standing on the edge grinning down at him over the stub snout of his revolver. Mead was on his back. He groped around for the rifle, knowing he had no time. No time to move, but lots of time to think. He noticed how steadily Burrows's extended arm held the gun as it pointed at him, moving slowly up his body. When it settled, Mead knew Burrows was going to shoot him in the forehead, just above the nose. He couldn't understand how the packets of soap powder were still standing upright in the kitchen cupboard. The wall had been torn away but the contents were undisturbed, poised precariously on the edges of the exposed shelves yet unmoved by the wind that had demolished the house. Miraculous!

'Drop it, Burrows!'

Mead heard the urgent shout and saw Burrows swing instantly to his left and fire in the direction of the voice. The second shot sounded almost simultaneously. The big man staggered back a couple of paces, half turned then pitched forward over the edge of the platform. As he disappeared from sight Mead heard his body thump on to the ground.

Someone was slapping his face. Mead opened his eyes and smiled up at Mike Lindsay.

'Never thought I'd be glad to see you again,' he said weakly.

Lindsay helped him to his feet, drawing his good arm round his shoulder to support him. Mead paused for a moment to look at the prostrate corpse spreadeagled in the wreckage.

'I only meant to wing the bastard,' Lindsay remarked as though annoyed with himself. 'Must be getting a little rusty.'

Mead stared at him, seeking the truth.

'Pity, that,' Lindsay added. His face gave nothing away.

Mead was surprised to see Karen still sitting in the car. She studied them anxiously as they approached.

'What's happened to him?'

'Dead,' Lindsay told her.

She said nothing, staring past them at the ruins.

When they reached the car door, Mead saw that she was handcuffed to the steering-wheel. A large crowd had gathered in the street and outside the front of the motel. Lindsay opened the car rear door and helped Mead get into the back seat.

'Mind your bum on the broken glass. You've already done enough damage to yourself to qualify for a place on an early flight out.'

He slammed the door and leaned in through the window.

'I'm going to get a car to run you up to the hospital, Mead. Meanwhile you can stay here and have a farewell chat with your girlfriend. You go away for a long time for running around with heroin in your suitcase.'

He turned to the crowd across the road.

'Someone get hold of a car, will you? We've got a wounded man here.'

A man stepped out of the crowd and walked rapidly towards the motel car park.

'Be with you in a minute,' he called.

Lindsay reached in through the car window and grabbed Mead by the ear jerking his head round to look at him.

'Mead, you got out of this lightly. All we can get you for this time is conspiring to export native fauna, which means that they won't even bother to put you in gaol where you belong.'

He tugged on the ear, making Mead wince.

'Take my advice. Make the most of the let-off. When you get back to Adelaide, make it up with your missus and stick to being a nice, honest truck driver if you're capable of it. You'll find life is much simpler that way.'

He paused to look down the street as a car approached,

then stuck his head back in the window and pressed the muzzle of his .38 firmly against Mead's temple.

'And if you ever run drugs again, I promise you I'll come back and personally finish off the job that Burrows began,' he said grimly.

In Lindsay's eyes that moment Mead saw the truth of Burrows's death.

About twenty light aircraft had been swept like leaves into a heap against a shattered iron hangar to the right of the main terminal building. Nearby a twin-engined plane was balanced against the hangar wall, its tail snapped off from the fuselage which was wedged inside the remains of the building to hold the aircraft poised on the broken stub of a wing, its undercarriage exposed. Others were strewn upside down across the tarmac between collapsed hangars and leaning floodlight posts.

Darwin's new million-dollar international terminal was a shattered ruin. Holes had been punched through the walls as though the building had been peppered with cannon-fire, dozens of the square sections of the suspended ceiling were missing and furnishings showered with plaster, insulation material and broken glass.

The building was no longer being used for the transit of refugees. On the first day of the airlift, panic had broken out as top-priority refugees, the sick, injured and pregnant and women and children, were crushed together by the pressure of the pushing crowd behind them. The lavatories were unusable and the packed terminal became fouled as the refugees waited for hours for aircraft to fly them out. The situation exploded when a party of Greeks hijacked an evacuation bus, drove straight out on to the tarmac and fought their way aboard a jumbo jet that had just rolled to a halt.

Trampling one another underfoot, the waiting refugees burst out of the terminal, broke through the police cordon and surrounded the big jet, refusing to move until it began to taxi.

The next day an army field radio network was established between the airport and the evacuation headquarters so that survivors arrived only when aircraft were waiting for them. The buses drove them from the evacuation centres at the suburban schools right up to the planes and unloaded their passengers alongside them.

When Frank Adams dropped Lindsay at the airport long lines of shabby refugees, clinging to the few personal possessions they had salvaged from the wreckage, were filing across the shimmering tarmac and up the steps of the waiting planes.

There were half a dozen large aircraft parked in front of the terminal and the air was full of the roar of engines. A British Airways jumbo was taxiing away for take-off as a Royal New Zealand Air Force Hercules touched down on the distant runway. The brightly-coloured assortment of commercial planes contrasted with the sombre grey of the services aircraft.

'What an operation!' gasped Adams. 'It looks more like Kennedy Airport than little old Darwin.'

Lindsay smiled and glanced up as another jet passed overhead.

'Twenty-five thousand people flown out in five days is not a bad effort, particularly when you can only use the airport during daylight,' Adams continued. 'I hear that one 747 went out with more than seven hundred on board.'

Lindsay lifted his suitcase from the back of the car and shook Adams's hand.

'When are you going to go, Frank?'

'Oh, I think I'll wait to see the fleet arrive. Once they

get started on the big clean-up, I'll probably take a trip down to Sydney to join the family. I won't be needed around here then for a while.'

'Be mad if you didn't seeing the Government's offering free return tickets. Be sure to look me up when you get to the big smoke.'

Adams nodded and watched Lindsay as he walked across to the chief marshal's table. The marshal glanced briefly at the docket Lindsay handed him and pointed towards a giant U.S. Air Force C141 with refugees filing up the loading ramp under its tail.

'Try the Starlifter,' he said wearily. 'They should be able to squeeze you aboard.'

The refugees were being let off the buses eight at a time, the number needed to fill a row across the floor of the great aircraft.

'Top priority five.' The loading marshal read aloud from Lindsay's slip of paper. 'Okay. You'll have to wait until we've loaded the buses coming for this one and we'll see if we can wedge you in as they close the door.'

He studied Lindsay curiously.

'We haven't loaded many fives,' he remarked as if to himself. 'There's still plenty of couples to come.'

Lindsay watched as group after group of shocked refugees filed past him and disappeared up the ramp. They were a mixed crowd with Indonesians, Malays, Chinese and European migrants liberally scattered amongst the Aborigines and white Australians. Despite the priority system there were many women, children and walking wounded who hobbled across the hot tarmac on rough sticks to be helped up the slippery steel ramp by one of the U.S. Air Force men. Silent adults had destination labels tied around their wrists and some of the youngsters had surnames and 'Sydney' painted on their brown arms and legs.

Every now and then the big negro sergeant controlling the flow from the top of the ramp would call out for a 'small one' to fit in the end of a row.

'We're going for a record,' he grinned down at Lindsay as though he felt he was owed an explanation. 'We got three hundred and sixteen out of Saigon in one lift, and I reckon we're going to beat that this time. It all depends on the size of their bums. Sometimes you can get ten in a row.'

Lindsay stood in the shade of the plane for more than an hour while bus after bus arrived, and other aircraft came and went. He was hot, tired and impatient to get back to Canberra, although he knew Karen would not appear in court there for at least two days and it would be weeks before the pilot was extradited from Bali.

At last the marshal put a final tick on his clip-board sheet.

'Okay, top priority five. That's the lot. Go on up and we'll pile the baggage in on top of you.'

The faces of the refugees filled the floor of the windowless fuselage. They were sitting facing the tail on blankets spread across the steel deck, cramped together shoulder to shoulder with knees tucked up in front of their chests to form back rests for the row in front. The most elderly and those with broken limbs had been allocated space on the only thing resembling a seat, the ledge running along the left-hand side of the aircraft. The opposite ledge was being used as a walk-way by crew members who were throwing webbing straps across the rows of raised knees and clipping them to the wall anchorages.

'Three hundred and nineteen,' the sergeant yelled to the marshal as Lindsay took his place on the floor in the rear row. 'I guess we can squeeze in two more if you can find them.'

A thin girl in Australian Air Force uniform was filling cardboard cups with milk which were passed along the rows to mothers holding babies. An American crewman handed out a few small cushions.

'We're sorry we can't make it more comfortable folks,' the sergeant apologised in a cheerful American accent. 'We did put in a hundred and fifty seats but we had to take them out to fit in some generators we've just brought in to give this place a bit of juice.'

He picked up a large brown-paper bag full of fruit and started tossing apples and oranges across the heads of the crowd.

'It's going to take us about five hours to get to Sydney. When we're airborne you'll probably be able to stand up and stretch your legs. There's one toilet down the front the women can use, and if you guys have to go we've got a bucket down the tail here behind the baggage.'

Lindsay was pouring orange juice from a plastic jerrican and passing the cups over his shoulder. After half an hour the last of the suitcases the buses had left on the tarmac were stacked on the loading ramp and secured in a net.

'Draw your feet back,' the sergeant ordered the rear row.

He jabbed a red button on the wall panel and the hydraulic ramp lifted the pile of baggage up into the fuselage at Lindsay's feet until a six-foot-high stack was sagging in the net above him. The heat and stench of unwashed bodies increased rapidly now that no fresh air was blowing into the plane.

A dog started yapping somewhere behind Lindsay as the aircraft began to move.

'Now, when we take off, folks, there's going to be a lot of noise, a lot of vibration and this whole place is going to fill with what you might reckon is smoke,' the sergeant told them. 'It's nothing to worry about when you see it coming out of those pipes up there. It's just refrigerated air, and it's all quite normal, so just hang on tight to those straps and you'll all be okay.'

The Starlifter was still for long minutes. A baby was crying, the only sound. Then a distant roar mounted to a thunderous din like the night of the cyclone.

'Here we go! Hang on!' shouted the sergeant, gripping a wall rail with both hands.

Lindsay slid across the vibrating floor until his feet were pressing against the pile of suitcases as white air hissed like steam from the pipes above his head. He felt the pressure of the knees in his back ease as the plane lifted from the runway.

The big negro gave a broad white grin.

'Smooth, man. Smooth.'

He clambered down from the ledge where he had hung on during take-off.

'Now, we'll soon have you in Sydney, and there's quite a reception waiting for you there, believe me. Food, clothes, beds. I reckon they are going to look after you folks like real V.I.P.s.'

He stretched up to peer out of a small porthole window as the plane banked.

'Jesus, that sure is a mess down there.'

He looked round at Lindsay.

'I guess you must be real glad it's all over.'

Lindsay smiled and settled back on the knees behind him.

Bernard Boucher was born in London, England, in 1934 and educated at the Royal Grammar School, Guildford. On completing National Service with the Royal Artillery in Gibraltar, he entered journalism as a reporter on the Surrey *Times,* Guildford, in 1955.

After travelling widely through Europe, including a six-month sojourn in Spain, he moved to Australia in 1965, where he now lives in Adelaide.

He gained prominence in Australian journalism as the "Man on the Spot" columnist for the Adelaide *Advertiser,* a job which took him to all parts of Australia, and occasionally overseas, covering many of the country's major news stories.

In September, 1978, he resigned from journalism to devote himself full time to writing novels.

The Megawind Cancellation has successfully launched him in his new career. He is now working on his second book.